BETRAYAL
A
Psychological Thriller

BETRAYAL

A Psychological Thriller

by

Lynn G. Armstrong

Text © 2025 by Lynn G. Armstrong

ISBN: 979-8-9893042-6-4

Cover art by Lynn G. Armstrong

Printed in the United States of America

CREATIONS BY LYNN

The Cabin

Betrayal: The act of disappointing a person's trust, hopes, or expectations.

Table of Contents

FOREWORD

By Peggy Brown, MSW

I knew the name Lynn Armstrong for some time, long before we ever met. Lynn was a friend of my sister, Patsy Taylor. It was Patsy who kept me current with Lynn's mid-life exploration of creativity through her painting and fiction writing.

I have now been in Lynn's company a number of times, and I marvel at the energy and focus she is able to call upon as she develops characters and plots for her books.

Betrayal: A Psychological Thriller is Lynn's fifth book. The setting is a psychiatric hospital built in the 1940s. While the grounds are well-maintained, the houses that serve as treatment centers on the large rural campus require repair. Treatment is offered for psychiatric illness and drug and alcohol addiction. Not infrequently, patients have lengthy hospital admissions. Extended care is based on the patient's need, not their ability to pay.

The reader is introduced to an array of characters, including patients and staff. The central character, whom we first meet, is Jennifer Nelson. She is a young adult ostensibly seeking treatment. We meet her in the dramatic Prologue when she is unconscious after eating a shrimp salad (she is dangerously allergic to shellfish) and having a near-death experience.

Jennifer is taken to the Emergency Department of a nearby general hospital, where she is successfully treated and kept overnight for safety. We meet Ben, a nurse who checks her orientation (What day is it? Who is our current president?). He provides Jennifer with a narrative of what happened while she was unconscious. This brief interaction lets the reader know that Lynn values the contribution of staff, which is generally not included. The nurse is one of a contingent of characters vigilant to Jennifer's safety.

Through a variety of experiences as a patient, the reader comes to see failures in the system of care and a foreshadowing of outright danger to Jennifer.

As the plot unfolds, we also witness Jennifer's deep commitment and tenacity in finding the truth.

I have intentionally not mentioned the medical staff's role in supporting Jennifer's reason for being admitted.

This is now the time for me to urge you to see what happens......Read the book!

Peggy Brown, LCSW, retired in 2023, is a licensed clinical social worker. She received an undergraduate degree in Psychology from Newcomb College and a master's degree in social work. She was the first social worker at the former Southern Baptist Hospital and later worked on an inpatient treatment unit for alcohol and drug abuse at JoEllen Smith Psychiatric Hospital. Most recently, Ms. Brown served as an advisor in Chevron's Employee Assistance Program. She also maintained a private practice in psychotherapy.

Other books by Lynn

Murder by Definition
Don't Forget the Butterflies
The Sword Cuts Both Ways
Julia's Odyssey

Dedication

To Jim and all those who have served their country, some of whom paid the ultimate sacrifice. We can never forget.

PROLOGUE

"Come on, Jennifer. Try eating a little something. You need your strength if you ever want to get well and leave this place. Your salad looks delicious, by the way."

No sooner had Jennifer taken a few bites of her salad than she felt her throat closing up and started choking. Within seconds, she was struggling to catch her breath. She lost consciousness immediately and slid to the floor. Just before she passed out completely, she could see the necklace her mom always wore dangling from her neck above her, catching the light. Was her mom here? Her next conscious thought was to see herself lying on the dining room floor from above, and Emily leaning over her and screaming for help. *How is this possible? Am I dead? Dear God, is that how I look?* What surprised her was how calm she felt, as if hovering over your body was a regular, everyday occurrence.

"Jennifer, are you all right? Help, someone, help! She's not breathing. I think she is dying. Call an ambulance."

The next time Jennifer opened her eyes, she sensed movement and saw fluorescent lights glaring down on her from above as she was being whisked down a long hall on a gurney. Her head was pounding, two IVs were connected to each of her arms, she was wearing a hospital gown, and was covered with a sheet.

"What happened? How did I get here?"

"Welcome back, Mrs. Nelson. I'm Ben," a young nurse said. "Apparently, you have a life-threatening allergy to shellfish, and you were eating a salad with shrimp in it when you went into anaphylactic shock, passed out, and fell on the floor. I can't believe you took a risk like that unless you didn't know your salad contained shrimp. You will probably have a king-size headache for a day or so. You are fortunate, Mrs. Nelson. Dr. Gallagher saved your life by retrieving your EpiPen from your purse, and you were transported by ambulance to the ER. We're taking you to your room now, and we'll probably keep you overnight as you took quite a blow to the head. You have a mild concussion, and we want to keep an eye on you for a few hours. Do you know what day it is?"

"Of course I do. It's Tuesday." Jennifer said.

"Who is our current president?"

"Donald Trump," she said, rolling her eyes.

"I'm sorry, Mrs. Nelson, but we will still need to keep you overnight to be on the safe side.

CHAPTER ONE
A Question of Legality

Carson, I want you to use your influence and connections as a psychiatrist at Heatherton Psychiatric Hospital and get me admitted as a patient. I'm going undercover until I can nail the murderers who killed my mother. My cover story will be that I'm writing a feature on Heatherton for The Times-Picayune. It might even give me 'story of the year' and make Pete Overton proud."

"Get you admitted as a patient? Jennifer, have you lost your mind? You can't be serious. You have no idea what you are asking. It would be helpful to put that out of your mind once and for all. You're obsessed. No one murdered your mother. Eileen died of natural causes. That crazy imagination of yours may make you an excellent reporter, but it certainly does the exact opposite in my world."

"I don't care. All I know is that the day before my mother died, we spent the whole day together, and she was fine. It was one of her better days. She was in a joyful frame of mind, and I washed and styled her hair. I took her to Heatherton's in-house salon, and she got a manicure and a pedicure. It was like old times. I had my mother back. The very next night, they called me and told me she had died in her sleep. Physically, she had no medical issues. I never wanted her to be put in that horrible place to begin with. The drugs her doctor put her on made her lethargic and more distant than ever from others. Most of the time, she was like a walking zombie. It didn't add up."

"I'm sorry you feel that way, Jennifer. It wasn't safe for her to live by herself anymore. It's been two years. I think you're still in serious denial. Don't forget that your mom suffered from depression and suicidal ideation for years. In her defense, she has been through a lot. Losing your father the way she did would derail anyone. Who would ever imagine your father would take his own life like that and leave your mother to find him? It was the epitome of selfishness. It didn't make any sense. His finances were in perfect order. He was in good health. Your mother was fortunate that his life insurance wasn't canceled, or she would have lost everything. I know it has been over a dozen years since that happened, but grief can take its toll on someone in different ways. Raising both of you girls by herself had to have been tough. When Dr. Denton diagnosed her with dementia, she wasn't on medication at the time; it became almost impossible to manage her care. If you recall, she left a saucepan on the stove, forgot about it, and nearly burned down her kitchen, not to mention the entire house. We hired a nurse to keep an eye on her, but she still managed to slip away; a neighbor recognized her and brought her home. The next time she wandered off, a policeman rescued her on the highway, and they both almost got hit by a car. We were lucky to get her admitted anywhere. Have you forgotten how shocked you were that the nursing homes wouldn't take her because of her aggressive behavior and hostile frame of mind? She was safe when she was at Heatherton. You're just in denial; you've always been that way when it comes to your mother."

Carson, that's your opinion, not mine. She was reacting to what was happening to her. Control of her own life was snatched away from her. That would make anyone aggressive. I only wish I had trusted my intuition and gotten a second opinion. Healthy women in their sixties don't die in their beds. Obviously, she wasn't safe at all because she was murdered. I was horrified at how Heatherton handled her body. Have you forgotten that when I went the following day to identify the body, they had already taken her to the morgue, and she had been cremated? How reliable is Dr. Denton? Is that even legal? Don't you have a problem with that?"

"No, I don't. Not if that's what she wanted, and I've known Brent Denton for years; he's a renowned physician in his field."

"Well, I do. As long as I can remember, my mother has always had her funeral planned down to her favorite hymns that she wanted sung at her funeral. Nothing was ever said about cremation. She had even picked out the dress she wanted to wear years ago. My mind is made up, and I'm not changing it. I will discover the truth if it's the last thing I do."

"Big surprise! Give me some time to think about it. You never listen to anything I say, once you've decided and dug your heels in."

Despite her frustration and his bull-headed manner, Jennifer had to chuckle to herself. From the moment she met Carson, she was captivated by his charm. It wasn't his intense, deep-set brown eyes or his six-foot-three countenance that gave people pause, but his larger-than-life personality. Carson Nelson wasn't a handsome man by his generational standards, but his colossal ego drew people to him like moths to a flame. Jennifer knew Carson had an enormous ego, and she fell head over heels in love with him way too fast for her liking. They met at a party at one of Carson's friends' homes; a family friend had invited her. Jennifer was in her junior year at a local college, and Carson was interning at Heatherton Psychiatric Hospital.

"Hello, I know you aren't one of Brian's friends. I would have remembered meeting you. Where have you been hiding all my life? Carson Nelson," he said, extending his hand.

Jennifer thought it was one of the cheesiest pickup lines she had heard in a while, but she wondered what this man's story was and why she was even interested in such an arrogant man. Perhaps it was true; opposites did attract, as he was unlike anyone she had ever met. She was sure his sexual masculinity and prowess, combined with his confident manner, were reeling her in faster than she had time to process.

"Jennifer Bastille, I'm here by the family's invitation."

Carson was an exceptional dancer, and the music was excellent. Eventually, they ended up on the terrace, talking for hours under the stars.

Chapter Two
The Cover Story

Jennifer, did you hear me? Where did you go? I will think about it. It won't be easy. You'll need to have someone on the inside to help you with this charade; otherwise, you could be at risk, and anything could happen. I'll talk to Tony. I can't make any promises. I wouldn't get my hopes up too high." Carson Nelson may have presented himself to others as the most confident, even arrogant, psychiatrist in his field, but all his colleagues and patients respected him. Still, under his well-constructed façade, like most of us, he had his own story. He came from poor beginnings due to an alcoholic father who never worked half the time. His father beat his mother regularly whenever he came home in a drunken stupor and continued to disrespect her by picking up women any time he felt like it, and made no effort to conceal it. Carson adored his mother and couldn't understand why she didn't take her son, leave, and never look back. He was shocked at how relieved he was when his father walked out one day and never looked back. He was in high school but worked after school, waiting tables at an upscale restaurant and running a paper route in the early morning hours. One night, he was waiting tables, and a child passed out and fell on the floor, choking. He'd taken a recent CPR class in high school, responded immediately, and saved the child's life. The child's parents were ecstatic. The incident profoundly affected him. Immediately, a dream took hold, and he swore to himself that he would somehow attend medical school, become a doctor, and never be poor again or endure the stigma that came with it. Two weeks later, his mother died in her sleep. The doctors said her heart just gave out. He was devastated but didn't even have time to grieve. He couldn't pay the rent; he had to let their house go. There was no way he could afford a funeral. He packed their few belongings the best he could and sold everything that was left at a garage sale. The state buried his mother, and he thought he would never get over the humiliation. He knew CPS (Child Protective Services) would try to grab him the first chance they got, as he was still a minor. He lied about his age, got another job waiting tables at a different establishment, continued his high school education, and lived out of his mother's car. With CPS on his heels, he was under continual stress, keeping up his grades and terrified they would catch up with him and he'd wind up in foster care.

"Carson, Mr. Turner is looking for you; he wants you in his office immediately. It sounds serious; what did you do this time?"

Carson knew Bart, his friend, was kidding, but he was still freaking out; his heart beating fast enough to hear it in his ears. He liked Mr. Turner. He was cool, but he was a guidance counselor. Why did he want to see him?

"Carson, come in. Please have a seat. I want to congratulate you on your outstanding GPA. I know you work after school and run a paper route in the mornings, and I realize what a challenge that must be for you. I'm beyond impressed and incredibly proud of you. I'm so sorry about the recent loss of your mother. Hear me out, son. I happen to know you are living out of your mother's car and dodging CPS. I wanted to discuss a proposal with you. Karen and I have an extra room; truthfully, you would be doing me a favor if you moved in with us. You are welcome to stay for as long as you like. I'm sure sleeping in a bed again would be more appealing than sleeping in a car. At least you wouldn't have to worry about CPS, and we wouldn't have to put up with Karen's pesky uncle whenever he's in town. What do you say? Are you okay? Do you need some water?" When he saw a tear roll down Carson's face, he didn't know what to do. Ken Turner didn't wait for an answer and was grateful for an excuse to quickly exit for some water. Carson moved in with Ken and Karen that weekend and was forever indebted to Ken Turner for his kindness. He stayed in touch with his mentor until Ken passed away several years later. He worked hard to maintain his grades and got into an Ivy League college with a scholarship. Ken lived long enough to see Carson graduate from medical school, start his internship at Heatherton Psychiatric Hospital, and even see Carson and Jennifer get married.

When Jennifer arrived at Heatherton Psychiatric Hospital and entered the long driveway surrounded by live oak trees on both sides, her first thought was that the massive, venerable buildings sprawled out before her on several acres had seen better days. The outsides of the buildings were in dire need of several coats of paint and attention. It was a huge campus, and it crossed her mind that getting lost could be easy for a newcomer like herself. In contrast, the grounds were well-maintained, and flowering plants of every color and description competed for their moment to shine.

"So, Jennifer, what inspired you to choose Heatherton Psychiatric Hospital, of all places, for research for a feature story? I am so sorry about the loss of your mother. We all loved Eileen; her passing away was a big shock." Jennifer was being interviewed in Dr. Anthony Gallagher's office at Heatherton Psychiatric Hospital for the first time. "When Carson told me what you wanted to do, I thought it was another example of his dry humor. I can put you in touch with a few patients to interview; alternatively, you can also speak with the staff. This is a psychiatric hospital, after all, and while many of our patients are relatively harmless, some are dangerous, especially to themselves and others. We take our security here very seriously, but it is not foolproof. We are determined to improve it, as patients can be very innovative and constantly look for new ways to escape, so we must always stay one step ahead of them. Are you sure you want to live here as a resident?"

"Yes, I do. I'm convinced my feature story would be more authentic if no one knew I was here from the paper. The residents would be more inclined to trust me if they identified me as a fellow patient."

Chapter Three
Jack Hale

Carson said you would say that. I can't say I didn't try. I assume you've noticed our buildings need some TLC, but please try not to judge. Heatherton was an absolute masterpiece in its day. Carson and I were proud to serve our internship here. The original hospital was built in 1942 and occupied 200 acres. In 2016, the state bought sixty acres. We are a psychiatric hospital as well as a rehabilitation facility for those with a drug or alcohol addiction. We work with the parish and even house the criminally insane. Unfortunately, some patients have been here for decades and may never be well enough to leave Heatherton. We actually have cabins here to help transition those who can eventually return to society, and it has been a very successful program. We are incredibly proud of its continued success. The cabins facilitate the transition by allowing patients to return to independent living whenever possible, while restoring their self-confidence as they reenter society. It is one of our most successful tools, devised by one of our very own doctors several years ago. The owners are debating whether to invest in costly renovations to restore Heatherton or sell and build elsewhere. Whatever they decide, I believe there is a real need for places like Heatherton. We take pride in providing a safe environment for our patients to live while they recover, enabling them to return to their families and eventually resume their everyday lives.

<hr>

Jennifer was always unprepared for the complete package that contained Anthony Gallagher, Carson's colleague, whenever she saw him, usually only at social functions. Tony and Carson had been friends since their college days. Not only was Tony beyond good-looking, but the sensuality surrounding him was distracting, and Jennifer struggled to focus. She suspected that he was completely unaware of his effect on women. He was of medium height with an athletic build, always tanned, as he loved the outdoors and any sport that was supported by the sun, with plenty of time spent in the water. However, his boyish features, sandy-colored hair, and azure eyes captivated women of all ages. Carson told her his patients adored him. His gentle nature had an instantly calming effect on his patients. Tony's relationship with his mother had a profound impact on his interactions with others. His father was killed in an industrial accident when Tony was ten. He was an only child. The plant where his father worked was found negligent due to several safety violations, and his mother received a substantial settlement from the company. As a result, they were set up financially for life.

Barbara Gallagher believed with all her heart "nothing ventured, nothing gained," and she ensured that her son shared this vital conviction. When Tony told his mother he wanted to be a doctor, she encouraged him to pursue anything and everything that would help him achieve his goal and fulfill his dream. She believed in her son and taught him the importance of believing in himself. Tony worked hard and was on the dean's list for three consecutive years. He met Carson in his junior year, and they became friends. They attended medical school together. When Carson started dating Jennifer, Tony was amazed by her beauty and mesmerized by her essence. While her luxurious, shoulder-length auburn hair surrounded her lovely face, and her thick lashes enhanced her hazel eyes, something else made his heart beat a little faster. It was her smile that took his breath away. A man would do anything for a smile like that. He'd never met anyone like her, but he quickly locked his feelings into a metaphorical box and never told anyone. He later met his beautiful wife, Rene, and loved her with every fiber of his being. It was a whirlwind courtship, and they were soon married. She was a gentle soul, and they both dreamed of having children one day. She had grown up as an only child, taught ballet at a dance studio, and had a passion for working with children. Then, one night, out of nowhere, she was showering and discovered a lump in her right breast. He found her crying in the bathroom. Even though his insides were churning, he did everything he could to support her emotionally. She was inconsolable. Two days later, her doctor confirmed their worst fears. Everything in their life was on speed dial after that. The chemo and radiation ravaged her body, leaving her weak and exhausted. It had already metastasized to other organs, and in six months, she was gone. He felt so helpless and angry. Rene never lost her faith in God, but he was furious with him. She died in his arms, and it was an hour before he could let her go and pull himself together enough to call an ambulance. He felt as if a part of him died with her.

⸙

"I'm impressed, Tony. I've heard about Heatherton through Carson all these years; Mother lived here then. Recently, I realized I've never seen any stories written about its history. It would make an excellent feature story and bring Heatherton's rich history back into the limelight where it belongs. I imagine there are probably people who aren't even aware that Heatherton exists or what role she plays in our community. Tony, I promise to do everything possible to give Heatherton the recognition she deserves."

"That would be great. It's about time Heatherton steps out into the limelight. I'm completely at your disposal. Just let me know how I can help."

Chapter Four
Jack's Perspective

Okay, Jennifer, against my better judgment, here's how it will go. You will need an assigned nurse, Edith Parker, at least on paper, to appear believable. Carson, Edith, and I will be the only ones who will know you are a plant. This is crucial for your safety. The fewer people who know, the safer you'll be. Come, I'll show you to your room. I'll assign you the same daily schedule as most of my patients, and hopefully, no one will be the wiser. You will eat meals in the dining room daily and attend group sessions with the other patients. I will be your assigned psychiatrist, as documented, and we will meet three times a week for sessions, just as I do with my other patients. This should expose you to lots of material for your article. However, you must never, under any circumstances, include patients' names or personal information in your feature story; their anonymity must always be protected. That means I must carefully review any content you wish to include in the article. You'll need to keep me updated periodically. The room Tony showed her was a little larger than she imagined it would be. Indeed, it was far beyond anything you would expect in a state hospital, but Heatherton served a wide variety of patients on a case-by-case basis. No one was turned away if they couldn't pay. She wasn't sure what her short stay would cost them, but she decided it was best to let Carson handle the financial aspect. There was a full-sized bed, an adequately sized television mounted on the wall, a bookcase, a nightstand, and an impressive, overstuffed, upholstered chair. A small closet and a four-drawer built-in chest of drawers were expected to hold her clothing. Jennifer immediately noticed her room's complete lack of mirrors and wondered how she could ever live with it. The room came with one window and a Roman shade. Venetian blinds were considered too risky and entirely out of the question. There was a private, generous-sized bathroom with only a shower.

"Most of our patients share a room, but that wouldn't be a good idea in your situation. You're fortunate we could find you something that affords you some privacy. I am sure more questions will arise, so please make a list, and we will review them during our private sessions. As if he had read her mind, he said, "I'm sure you've noticed the lack of mirrors for obvious reasons. Of course, you may have a mirror, but please keep it out of sight for the safety and respect of others. I would encourage you to call me if you have something that won't wait. Please use discretion when making calls, as some patients aren't allowed to have cell phones. Guard yours with your life. You don't want to draw attention to yourself or do anything that will blow your cover. I will send Edith, your assigned nurse, to your room soon so you can meet her. She has already been briefed. Housekeeping should be bringing in your linens and toiletries soon. I'm afraid the doors have no locks, but you are in one of the safer wards, and the halls are monitored nightly. Most wards can only be entered or exited using a keypad. If the absence of locks freaks you out, you can always put a chair against your door, but it might glean the ire of the rest of the staff as they have no idea of the real reason you're here. It would be advisable for you to leave any valuables at home. I'll send someone from the maintenance department here to assign a lock to your nightstand drawer, but I'm afraid that's the best I can do. The patients on this ward do not pose a threat but can occasionally be a nuisance. I'll leave you to get settled. The day room is located down the hall from you, where most patients spend their free time. It features large windows that bring in ample light, making it an excellent spot for reading. The grounds here are lovely; be sure to explore them at your earliest opportunity. Get some rest. You'll need it, Jennifer. You'll be expected to be in the dining room at 7:30 sharp for breakfast tomorrow. You have a meeting with me at 11:00, lunch at 12:30, and group at 2:30. Good luck, and we'll talk tomorrow. Do you have any idea how long you'll be staying?"

"As long as my research takes, I guess. Tony, don't worry, I'll be fine."

Tony wished he were as confident as Jennifer was regarding her safety. It was a psychiatric hospital, after all, and sometimes an unpredictable environment. Carson was crazy. If she were his wife, he would be terrified. Of course, Carson wasn't like everybody else; never had been.

Jennifer was barely awake at 7:20 when she entered the dining room for breakfast. She hadn't rested well the night before; she tossed and turned for hours, and morning came too early. She jumped when someone with a cane lightly touched her elbow as she passed him. "Hi, it's Harry Mason." I don't think you remember me, do you?"

"No, I'm sorry, I don't think we've ever met. I'm Jennifer Nelson."

Harry Mason, a short, stout, stocky man with a ruddy complexion, glared up at her. I saw you here several times last summer. You've fixed your hair differently, but I never forget a face. We spoke briefly a couple of times. I remember you. It's not as if I was hallucinating. Who's your nurse?"

"Edith Parker."

"Oh, that one. Be careful. If she had her way, she'd have us all walking around like a bunch of drugged zombies, and she'd have more time to hang out in Dr. Nelson's office, if you know what I mean.

"I'm sorry, I guess I forgot Mr. Mason. Thanks for the caveat, though, about Ms. Parker. As Dr. Gallagher warned, Jennifer decided it was best not to draw any attention to herself. She assumed complacency was the safest way to achieve that as Harry stormed off to find a table to await his breakfast. She found a table and sat down; someone brought her a plate. She was surprised that the scrambled eggs, bacon, toast, and orange juice were actually palatable. She ate quietly and decided to check out the day room as she was free until her session with Dr. Gallagher at eleven. The day room was huge and painted in a soft light mauve, which she assumed was designed to create a calm and serene background for the patients. She tried not to think about the bars on the windows. Small, intimate circles of tables encouraged conversation throughout the room. Some patients were playing games, someone was playing the piano in the far corner, and one gentleman was staring blankly at the TV, but Jennifer seriously doubted whether he saw or heard what he was looking at. She tried to concentrate on a magazine she had picked from one of the heavy wire racks that bolted to the wall, but quickly realized it was an exercise in futility.

Chapter Five
Edith Parker

Mrs. Nelson, I don't think we've met before. I'm Edith Parker. I'm your assigned nurse for the duration of your stay. I'm sorry I didn't make it to your room yesterday. I'm so pleased to meet you," she said, extending her slender hand with beautiful, long, brilliant, red-painted fingernails. I hear you are researching a feature article on Heatherton. What a surprise. I can't imagine anything your readers would like to read about here. I assume Tony has informed you of the importance of privacy. It is crucial, you understand." Even though Ms. Parker had a radiant smile, her eyes reflected the opposite. Jennifer could feel the iciness behind the smile that separated them. Edith Parker's physical appearance was outwardly breathtaking, with her luxurious shoulder-length blond hair and brown eyes, and she had a figure to die for. Still, Jennifer could only sense a small glimpse of the real Edith Parker. Beneath the beautiful façade lay a cold and heartless woman, incapable of genuine emotion, who would do anything to achieve her goals. Even enduring their most debilitating illnesses, the patients intuitively sensed her enigmatic coldness and feared her and avoided her whenever possible. When Edith Parker was born, it was definitely into a world she would never understand. She was an only child and an heir to the Parker empire. The Parkers came from old money and had never worked a day in their entitled lives. While they lavished more toys and things on Edith than she could ever want or need, they never gave her what she needed the most: their love. She was raised by nannies who were well-chosen for their credentials, not their capacity for love. Her parents saw that she attended the best boarding schools. Unfortunately, by the time Edith was an adult, she would spend most of her life looking for love in all the wrong places. Whenever she exited one empty relationship, another was waiting in its place.

"Jennifer, are you settling in okay?" Let me know if you need anything. I have a meeting in ten minutes. I apologize. We will talk soon."

"No, thank you, Edith, I'm fine." The woman made her skin crawl for some reason, not even waiting for an answer. *Was there anything to what Harry Mason insinuated? Was Edith Parker after her husband?* Edith Parker seemed to be on a mission and hurried off so fast that Jennifer wondered why she even approached her in the first place.

Well, aren't we going to have fun with that one? What could Carson and Tony be thinking of anyway? A feature article on Heatherton for The Times-Picayune? Really? Tony probably believes in her little façade, but Carson is no fool. I don't dare take my eyes off that one for a minute until I figure out what she's up to.

"So, Jennifer, how is your first day at Heatherton going so far?"

"Okay, I guess. It is certainly an adjustment. I definitely need to stay focused on why I'm here in the first place," she said.

Dr. Gallagher closed the door and sat down behind his massive mahogany desk. On his desk, an 8x10" picture of him smiling with his arm around a beautiful woman with long auburn hair, blue eyes, and a radiant smile on her face was on display. Jennifer had forgotten how beautiful Rene, his wife, was, and would never forget how devastated Tony was when she died after only a year of being diagnosed with breast cancer. Carson told her that Tony was so consumed by grief when his wife died, he took six months off to get his head on straight. Three years had passed since cancer had stolen Rene from him, and he never talked about her.

"I did meet a strange little man who swore he had seen me here before. I confess it unnerved me a bit. He was adamant that he knew me and seemed agitated that I didn't remember him. I'm fairly certain I never met him when Mother was here. He even insinuated that I thought he was hallucinating."

"Don't tell me, that would be Harry Mason. He's completely harmless, I assure you. He has macular degeneration, among other medical issues, and his vision is severely compromised. He wasn't being paranoid. I'm surprised he told you as much as he did. He also has trust issues. When one faces blindness, it's not uncommon to experience hallucinations. He suffers from (CBS) or Charles Bonnet Syndrome. Charles Bonnet was a naturalist and philosopher of the eighteenth century. When his eyesight began to fail, Charles Bonnet began to study and chronicle the brain's efficacy in the face of blindness. At the same time, Charles Bonnet's knowledge of biology was limited. However, his works are often referred to even today as a diagnostic tool. Harry's hallucinations are not psychotic, but the brain's reaction to the loss of sight. It's almost as if the brain can't accept that the eyes can no longer see and substitutes false images that are only relevant to the individual. The individual usually recognizes that the images are unreal and learns to live with them. It's a sensitive subject for him and has nothing to do with you, I assure you. I'm sorry if he upset you. You'll get used to Harry and the other residents on this ward after you've been here for a while."

"I've also noticed an elderly man staring off into space most of the time. He doesn't seem able to talk with anyone, which is sad. I've noticed him in the halls sometimes. I realize you can't divulge anything for obvious reasons, but I was just concerned."

"I hear you. That's correct. I can tell you what everyone here knows: he is old enough to have endured a lobotomy that went bad. Thank God they aren't doing them anymore. However, he is harmless, like Harry. His family brought him here years ago; he had nowhere else to go."

"A lobotomy. I certainly hope not. I don't know anything about the procedure, but the abuse I've heard that surrounds the procedure is terrifying."

"That is understandable. I feel the same way. A well-documented case occurred in 1953. They referred to him only as Patient H.M. to protect his anonymity. The patient suffered from severe epileptic seizures and underwent a radical new procedure. Unfortunately, a twenty-seven-year-old factory worker at the time, H.M., left the operating room with complete amnesia and was unable for the rest of his life to form any long-term memories. For the next sixty years of his life, he became one of the most studied people in the history of neuroscience and taught us much of what is known today about memory. What is so egregious is that he was used like a guinea pig or a lab rat after an aunt, his only living relative, died. He didn't have the emotional intelligence to stand up against the doctors who were exploiting him for their gratification. He no longer had anyone to care for him and was moved to an institution where he lived for the rest of his years, enduring countless interviews and tests, which he complied with because he didn't have the mental capacity to understand it was his decision, and he didn't have to. Tragically, after he died, doctors were grappling over his brain, supposedly to use it in the name of science."

"Unbelievable. The poor man. I'm sure glad they don't do that anymore."

"Indeed, there were many horrific procedures done in the fifties and sixties supposedly in the name of science that were an abomination, and thousands of innocent patients suffered at the hands of the doctors who perpetuated them. Lobotomies, ice baths, and electroconvulsive shock treatments were some of the worst. Perhaps, one day, psychiatric hospitals like Heatherton will help eliminate some of the stigma that these procedures have left behind. A handful of doctors were among the first to arrive when Heatherton opened, caring for their patients with compassion and respect. Since then, doctors and staff have been carefully picked to perpetuate what they started. When the community sees patients improve and return home to their families, we hope to be viewed more positively and ultimately recognized as a place of healing one day. Unfortunately, it may take years for Heatherton's reputation to become the norm rather than the exception in our community."

Chapter Six
Meeting More Patients

This is entirely off the subject, but what do you
know about Dr. Denton?"
"He is one of our best doctors on staff. His
grandfather, Dr. Henry Denton, was one of the first
doctors to practice at Heatherton, and the legacy he left
behind is unequaled. If I remember correctly, he was on
our ethics board here for years. He was your mother's
doctor, wasn't he? Why do you ask?"

"No reason in particular. I've heard the patients here
talk about him. I was just wondering if you knew him. I'd
better get going. It's been great, Tony. I appreciate all
the information."

Jennifer was on her way to group therapy when she
noticed a thin, disheveled woman, possibly in her early
thirties, with straw-like blond hair from a botched do-it-
yourself bleach job, shuffling straight towards her.
"Hello, I'm Maggie. You're new here, right?" Are you on

your way to a group therapy session? Watch out for the minions; they're everywhere."

"Excuse me?"

"You know the flatterers and clowns who speak out of both sides of their mouths that will say anything to get you to spill the beans. Don't fall for their bologna if you don't want them in your business. The next thing you know, they'll have you on the drug of the week here, and you'll be running around in a fog like the rest of us."

"Okay, I appreciate it, Maggie." Maggie Thorne was a sweet, confused, and harmless young woman whom her doctors and fellow patients loved. She had lived at Heatherton for the last five years since her husband died of pancreatic cancer, and shortly after, she lost her daughter, her only child of six. Mourning her losses was a nightmare for her, and she was never herself again. With no family left or few friends who could care for her, she was eventually admitted to Heatherton when she was found wandering alone in the neighborhood at all hours of the night. Her doctors said it wasn't safe for her to live by herself. Later, they suspected Maggie's newfound contentment and comfort at Heatherton was because she had finally come to terms with her loneliness and had become one of their model patients. "Come on, you can sit by me," she said in a conspiratorial tone, shuffling to the nearest chair by the door. Jennifer immediately noticed a beautiful girl, two chairs down from them, slumped in her chair, crying softly to herself. She was surprised that no one even seemed to notice. It was a medium-sized room with at least a dozen chairs arranged in a half circle, with Dr. Gallagher seated in the middle.

"Everyone, we would like to welcome our newest person to Heatherton." Her name is Jennifer Nelson. You may have seen her recently in the hall or day room, so please make her feel welcome. Remember, we were all new here once and know what it feels like. Who wants to begin? Whitney, can you tell us what your weekend with your parents was like? Whitney was a beautiful young woman of twenty who had studied ballet since she was ten and suffered from bulimia and body dysmorphia. When she looked in the mirror, she saw an obese woman with a horrible complexion and ears too large for her face. She was constantly obsessed with what she perceived as her ugly flaws, even though people often told her how beautiful she was. Whenever she went home for a weekend to see her parents, her mother in particular, whom she could never please, she always came back depressed and in worse shape than she was when she left. She had performed in the theatre countless times, but would always be up the night before vomiting and with diarrhea from the sheer terror of performing before a live audience whom she perceived to be judgmental. It would take years to undo the damage her domineering and obsessive mother had done. Dr. Gallagher's biggest concern was that Whitney Thorne would get sucked into the plastic surgery nightmare so many, including her mother, had before her, ruined their looks, and then couldn't get off the addictive roller coaster, always believing another surgery could make them more beautiful.

"It was okay, I guess. I think my mother is more interested in whether I've been doing my stretches or gaining a couple of pounds than she is in seeing me for a visit."

"Jack, how was your weekend?" Getting Jack to participate in the group was a challenge, but Dr. Gallagher continued to try, always hoping he would open up one day. Jack Hale had been a patient at Heatherton for five years and was still listed as a suicide risk. He was a Vietnam veteran and one day was found living under a bridge on the edge of town, malnourished, severely dehydrated, and disoriented. He was immediately taken to the New Orleans Veterans Hospital. After being placed on IVs for a couple of days and evaluated, a psychiatrist on duty that night assessed him and deemed him to have the most severe case of post-traumatic stress disorder (PTSD) he had ever seen in twenty-five years of practice. Dr. Long ached for the older man. His eyes reflected his pain. Jack Hale had been a helicopter pilot in South Vietnam, and one fateful day, his world changed forever. He was copiloting with Tim Allen, his commanding officer. As they were ascending, Jack hollered out. "Look out! Incoming! Incoming trees ahead!" They crashed, and a tree struck the windshield, causing the rotor blade to shatter through it. He quickly shut down the engine before he passed out. When he came to, he was in a Medivac, and there was a body bag on the floor less than ten feet in front of him. Some crazy fool hadn't zipped it up correctly, and when the Medivac suddenly lurched, a head covered in purple phosphorus from the flare that had gone off when they crashed rolled out at his feet. His C.O., with whom he had been sitting in the cockpit not an hour before, had been decapitated, and for the rest of his life, he was visited in his nightmares by the 'purple head,' insisting it was Jack who should have died. No amount of medication could manage his survivor's guilt. Twice, he tried to drown out the demands of his accuser by taking a bottle of pills, but somehow survived, eventually lost the only woman he ever loved, sabotaged every job he ever had since the war, and finally became another statistic of homeless vets.

"Not today," he said, jumping up and heading for the door.

"Okay, guys, let's wrap it up early today." After Jack's explosive exit, Dr. Gallagher knew the rest of the hour would be an exercise in futility as most of the patients knew who Jack was and felt a profound empathy for him whenever he had a psychotic meltdown.

It was still a little early, and Jennifer didn't feel like going back to her room, so she decided to grab something to read in the day room, but struggled to focus when she noticed the older man from their group session, who had left in a hurry, staring out the window. He must have sensed her gaze upon him. "What are you looking at, lady?"

"I'm sorry, I guess I was just concerned. Are you okay?"

"I know who you are. I saw you in Dr. Gallagher's group session. You're a newbie here. There's nothing you can do. It's not your problem now, is it? We all have our demons, don't we? Isn't that why we're here in the first place?"

"Of course, but sometimes it helps to have someone to connect with."

"Lady, I promise you, you wouldn't want to connect with me once you got to know me. That's a fact."

"Jennifer Nelson, Jack Hale, isn't it?" Jennifer reached out to shake his hand, and for a brief second, she thought she saw something in the man's eyes, like a glimmer of hope, and then it was gone. Jack was a tall, lanky, lean man with the most incredible, sad, green eyes she'd ever seen. She thought she had heard someone say he was a Vietnam veteran, so that would put him in his mid-to-late sixties, but he looked much older. Despite the wear and tear on his face and salt and pepper hair, she knew instinctively there was a man in there somewhere, a wounded soul who was worth knowing, but someone who had learned to use his pain to distance himself from others. She hoped to have time to befriend him during her short stay. If he had been a Vietnam veteran, only God knew what horrible pain he carried behind those sad eyes, and he probably could use a friend. Obviously, a friend was the last thing on his mind this morning as he ignored her extended hand and wandered off to stare at the television again. She was here to discover what had happened to her mother, but the reporter in her was intrigued by the people she had already met who tugged at her heart, and now this troubled soul was no exception.

Just what I need: another bleeding heart. Is there no end to the supply? Where do they all come from anyway? Don't they realize what I need the most is to be left alone?

⁓

Jennifer had some free time on her schedule, so she decided to visit the beautiful outdoor courtyard. She grabbed a drink from one of the vending machines in the foyer and headed outside. She loved the impeccable grounds and the expansive assortment of colorful flowers everywhere. She found a bench and was settling into her book when she realized someone was walking up.

"Hello, I see you are enjoying our beautiful grounds. Mind if I join you?"

"Not at all, please sit."

"I'm Barbara Turner," she said, extending her hand. "I've meant to introduce myself and welcome you to Heatherton, Jennifer. I'm a CNA here. How are you doing so far?"

Chapter Seven
Emily Pettito

Jennifer immediately noticed that Barbara Turner was a genuine person whose authenticity must have been greatly appreciated by both patients and staff alike. She was a petite young woman with a pixie cut that perfectly suited her heart-shaped face, making her warm brown eyes stand out. With her floral scrubs and petite frame, people often underestimated her when they first met her. She loved her patients and treated everyone with the same kindness. However, she could be a force to be reckoned with if the need arose, especially when she saw anyone mistreating a patient, and Lord help you if it was one of hers.

"I think I'm adjusting well enough to the routine, thank you. People are remarkably friendly here. I've made some friends. Did you happen to know Eileen Bastille, who used to live here at Heatherton? She passed away some time ago, but I hear the patients talk about her sometimes. She was a cousin to a good friend of mine."

I knew of her. She had dementia, I believe, but she wasn't one of my patients. Who's your nurse?"

"Edith Parker."

"Okay. Edith was also Ms. Bastille's nurse. She's probably the one who could answer your questions, except for anything that would violate privacy guidelines. I enjoyed meeting you, Jennifer. You're not on my floor, but if I can ever be of any help, please don't hesitate to let me know."

⁂

"Miss, do you know Jesus?"

"Excuse me." Jennifer looked down at a petite young woman with shoulder-length dark brown curly hair, warm brown eyes, and a big smile to match.

"I'm Emily Pettito, but you can call me Emmy; all my friends do. I asked you if you knew Jesus. Don't be scared; I'm quite harmless. I might have my problems, but knowing Jesus is what will help get me out of this place. That's a fact."

Jennifer didn't know Emily's story, but immediately connected with her. Perhaps her warm demeanor drew her in as she looked at you through warm brown eyes when you spoke, as if getting to know you was the most important thing on her radar then. She guessed Emily Pettito to be in her mid-to-late thirties, a careful dresser with dark, curly, shoulder-length hair and a slight build of medium height who barely tipped the scales at 105 pounds.

"You're Jennifer Nelson, the new girl, aren't you? I've seen you in Dr. Gallagher's group sessions before. Any relation to Dr. Nelson?" Suddenly, a chair flew across the room and crashed near them, followed by a guttural scream. She saw Jack Hale drop to the floor, crawl on all fours, and wedge his lanky body under a pool table as far back as he could.

"Don't worry, he'll be all right. Jack does this every so often. The poor man suffers from post-traumatic stress disorder (PTSD). He was a decorated officer in the army and flew helicopters during the Vietnam War. God only knows the horrors he suffered. Thank goodness, Dr. Gallagher is his doctor. If Dr. Gallagher can't help him, then no one can break through the wall he has built around himself." Two bulky orderlies attempted to coax him out from under the pool table until they could get close enough to administer a sedative. Jack was curled up tightly in an embryonic ball, his head tucked in like a turtle. Finally, they were able to administer a sedative to him. The orderlies carried him out on a stretcher when it kicked in. It upset and distracted Jennifer so much that she suddenly realized Emily was tapping her on the arm.

"Come on, dear, let's go get lunch. There's nothing we can do for Jack now. The first group always gets the best choices." The last thing Jennifer wanted was food, but she let Emily hold her hand and lead her to the dining room.

"Come on, Jennifer. Try eating a little something. I promise you they will take good care of Jack. The Vietnam War took a toll on him, but he's a resilient old guy, and he'll probably be back here tomorrow. You need your strength if you ever want to get well and leave this place. Your salad looks delicious, by the way."

No sooner had Jennifer taken a few bites of her salad than she felt her throat closing and started choking. "Help me, I can't breathe," she gasped as she immediately slid to the floor. Just before she passed out completely, she could see the necklace her mom always wore dangling from her neck above her, catching the light. *Was her mom here?* The next conscious thought she had was of looking down at her body on the dining room floor from above, and Emily screaming for help. *How is that possible? Am I dead? Dear God, is that what I look like?* What surprised her was how calm she felt, as if hovering over her body was a regular, everyday occurrence.

"Jennifer, are you all right? Help, someone, help! She's not breathing. I think she is dying. Call an ambulance."

The next time Jennifer's eyes opened, she sensed movement and saw fluorescent lights glaring down on her from above as she was being whisked down a long hall on a gurney. Her head was pounding, IVs were connected to both of her arms, she was wearing a hospital gown, and covered with a sheet.

"What happened? How did I get here? Am I in a hospital?"

"Welcome back, Mrs. Nelson," a young nurse said. "I'm Ben Husser. I was on call when you were brought in. You have a life-threatening allergy to shellfish, and you were eating a salad with shrimp in it when you went into anaphylactic shock, passed out, and fell on the floor. I can't believe you took such a risk unless you were unaware your salad contained shrimp. You will probably have a king-size headache for a day or so after falling. You are fortunate, Mrs. Nelson. Dr. Gallagher saved your life by retrieving your EpiPen from your purse and taking you to the ER. We're taking you to your room now, and we'll probably keep you overnight as you took quite a blow to the head. You have a mild concussion, and we want to keep an eye on you for a few hours. Do you know what day it is?"

"Of course I do. It's Tuesday." Jennifer said.

"Who is our current president?"

"Donald Trump," she said, rolling her eyes.

"We'll still need to keep you overnight, Mrs. Nelson, to be on the safe side.

<hr/>

"Jennifer, if you don't stop this insane idea of yours, I will. Thank God Tony was making rounds and in the hall outside the dining room when he heard a patient screaming bloody murder when you hit the floor, or we'd be planning your funeral."

"Don't be so dramatic, Carson. Nothing has changed. I'm not leaving. It's not even open for discussion. I am still trying to find out what happened to my mother. I have gotten a lot of good information for my article on the paper, but that's all so far. It was supposedly an unfortunate accident. My nurse, Edith Parker, was supposed to have alerted the kitchen of my shellfish allergy. I don't like her, and I'm sure the feeling is mutual. I don't trust her either."

"There you go, off and running with that imagination of yours again. Now, who's being dramatic? Surely, you're not blaming Edith Parker for what happened. You said yourself it was an accident. I give up; you never listen. Do your thing, Jennifer, like you always do, but don't expect me to be there to pick up the pieces when everything backfires on you. I won't relax until you return home. Give up this harebrained idea of yours so things can return to normal. You realize I won't even be able to keep an eye out for you as I'm leaving in the morning for a medical conference in Atlanta. I'll be gone for a week." *I can't wait. She is just like her mother; no one can tell her anything. She'll find out someday how foolish she is if she doesn't get herself killed first.*

Unfortunately, a dripping cynicism had become integral to Carson's banter lately and had become his new normal. Most of the time, Jennifer could tune it out and ignore him because of his background, but it was still a challenging and caustic environment she didn't want to be in anymore. Periodically, she tried to remind herself that his alcoholic father had deserted him and his mother after many years of physical and mental abuse. He worked tables at a busy restaurant after school and had a paper route in the morning. His mother worked two jobs and took in ironing to make ends meet. In his sophomore year, his mother died in her sleep. The doctors said her heart just gave out. As he was still a minor, he found another job, lied about his age, and dodged CPS daily. He was living out of his mother's car when a benevolent school counselor took him into his home until he could enter college. He remained a fixture in Carson's life until he died. Jennifer had learned long ago that Carson's arrogance was a façade he used as a protective mechanism to hide his insecurities. *What was wrong with her lately?* Something had changed, and she was afraid it was her. She had entirely lost her objectivity with Carson.

"I didn't say that, Carson. There is something about Edith Parker that I can't quite put my finger on. If it's the last thing I do, I'll get to the bottom of it." She ignored Carson's scowl and obvious irritation.

⁂

"Jennifer, are you okay? You gave us quite a scare. Come on, let me buy you a cup of coffee." Tony led her to an empty table closer to the back of the dining room.

"Tony, did I flatline?"

"Flatline? "You scared me within an inch of my life. When I heard Emily screaming and saw you on the floor, I couldn't detect a pulse, and you were unconscious. Emily said you were eating when you started choking and said you couldn't breathe, pointed to your purse, and then passed out. I have a nephew with a peanut allergy and am familiar with life-threatening allergies, so I looked in your purse and found your Epi pen. By the time the ambulance got here, you were breathing okay, but you still seemed a little out of it, so they took you to the hospital. As the ENT explained, sometimes the epinephrine can wear off, and you might need another injection to make it to the hospital."

"Tony, do you want to hear something weird? You'll think I'm crazy. One minute, I was at the table choking, struggling to breathe, and then I was looking down at my body on the floor, still hearing Emily screaming, all from somewhere near the ceiling. Before I passed out, I thought my mom was leaning over me; I saw the necklace she always wore catching the light, dangling over me. I saw you rush in and ask Emily what happened. You wore a light blue dress shirt and a tie with navy blue pants, and you weren't wearing your doctor's coat. Then, the next thing I knew, I was awake and lying on a hospital gurney, being wheeled down the hall by somebody named Ben to my room."

Chapter Eight
A Scary Experience

That is weird but not crazy. That's uncanny. Would you believe I spilled coffee on my coat that morning and got so busy that I never got to the laundry to get a clean one? As a matter of fact, I was on my way to doing just that when I heard Emily screaming. I don't think you're crazy at all, Jennifer. You didn't have a pulse, and you weren't breathing. The epinephrine is what brought you back. Out-of-body experiences during extreme trauma, clinical death, and numerous other occurrences are documented in medical journals all over the world and are more common than you'd think. That's a fact. Countless people have shared detailed reports that can't be scientifically explained while experiencing an out-of-body experience. Seeing your mom is not entirely impossible when you are having an out-of-body experience. I appreciate you sharing this with me. It's a fascinating subject, and I'd love to explore it with you sometime. Unfortunately, I have a board meeting in five minutes. I hope you've replaced your EpiPen. It saved your life. You are lucky to be here. Promise me, you'll take better care of yourself."

⚬⚭⚬⚭⚬

"Jennifer, you're back. I was so worried about you. When you fell on the floor, I thought you had died. I prayed for you. What happened? You can't put much stock in what you hear around here."

"Thank you, Emily; I appreciate your concern. I'm sure your prayers helped. I have a life-threatening allergy to shellfish. The kitchen is supposed to have that information and be on high alert, but obviously, someone made a mistake. I'm okay now, thanks to Dr. Gallagher. He grabbed my EpiPen from my purse, and thanks to your screaming for help. Both of you saved my life."

"Anytime, you scared me to death. That was a crazy day. If you remember, Jack flipped out in the day room, and they carried him out on a stretcher just before you hit the floor in the dining room."

"Emily, on a completely different subject, did you know Eileen Bastille?" She used to be a patient here."

"Of course, I knew Eileen. She was my dear friend. Why do you ask?"

"Just curious, I guess. I overheard some patients talking about her in the day room the other day."

"I'm sure you did. Everyone is still talking about the mystery surrounding her death. I loved her. We were kindred spirits. I think she had a gift. People were drawn to her, including me. Most of us here are broken; you always felt much better just being around her. When I was young, I had an abortion. In those days, having a baby out of wedlock automatically made you a social outcast. David and I were only seventeen, and his parents refused to let him see me. My parents were more concerned about what people would say, so they took me to live with an aunt with the understanding that I would have an abortion. I never spoke to them after that. My aunt was a bitter spinster and never learned how to love. I couldn't grow up in that kind of environment, and as soon as I recovered enough, I ran away. I was a minor living on the streets when I met Dr. Gallagher; he bought me dinner one evening, and the rest is history. When I confided in Eileen, she never judged me and loved me unconditionally for who I am."

"She gave me this," she said, pulling a heart with a diamond in the middle on a gold chain from her blouse. Emily was wearing her hair piled on top of her head, which flattered her heart-shaped face. As she held the heart pendant out for Jennifer to see, the chain caught on a mass of curls that immediately escaped and hung in curly tendrils around her neck.

Jennifer gasped. "That is a beautiful necklace. May I?" she asked. She picked up the heart with the diamond in the middle of Emily's neck and turned it over. When she saw the minute imperfection on the back of the heart, barely visible to the naked eye, she was covered with goosebumps and thought her legs might give out from under her any minute. It was her mother's necklace. Suddenly, Jennifer realized that what she thought she saw before she passed out was her mom's necklace hanging from Emily's neck, not her mother's.

"Jennifer, you look like you've seen a ghost. Are you okay?"

"Yes, I'm fine; I should have eaten breakfast this morning. Your friend must have cared deeply for you to have given you such a beautiful necklace. That's quite an impressive diamond.

"I always admired it, so I was shocked when she insisted on giving it to me as a token of our friendship. Eileen was such a Godly woman. She said every time I looked at it, she wanted me to remember that God loved me and that all things are possible through him. I'm convinced that without her, I would never have been able to forgive my parents and heal. I never take it off. I hide it inside my clothes as I am paranoid that someone will want to steal it. You can tell it is valuable. You know how things are around here. There was a rumor circulating at Heatherton for a while that it was stolen, but I've no idea how that got started since you're the only person I've ever told I had it. Do you think she knew she was going to pass away? She supposedly had dementia, but Edith Parker is her nurse, and everyone here knows she over-sedates her patients. No one will ever snitch on Ms. Parker for fear of retaliation. We ate together daily, and I would visit her whenever she had an off day. Of course, they say she also suffered from depression, but when she didn't swallow her pills, if Edith wasn't looking, she was a different person. I don't think she needed them. We all know that if you take a psychotic person off their meds, they immediately go bonkers. When she wasn't full of that garbage, she was herself and fine. I heard the night she died that her daughter spent the whole day with her. She talked of nothing but the anticipated day for a week; we were all aware of it. She was so excited and ensured she didn't swallow her medicine that morning to enjoy her daughter's visit. Then, the next day, we heard she died in her sleep. It doesn't make any sense. She was barely in her sixties. Except for all the drugs they had her on, I don't think she had any health issues. I'll always believe she was misdiagnosed. She was like a zombie most days. We have an in-house clinic, and I don't remember the last time anyone took her for a checkup, but someone always made sure she never ran out of her medication, if you know what I mean. I don't know what they gave her. Still, knowing Edith Parker, it was probably strong enough to slow a semi down, let alone a tiny thing like Eileen." Emily looked nervously over her shoulder to see if anyone was listening. "I'm sorry, I need to go. I don't want to miss Law and Order. I'm so glad you're okay," she said giving Jennifer a big hug.

Life at Heatherton picked up where it had left off before Jennifer had an anaphylactic reaction to the shrimp in her salad. Jennifer continued to work diligently on her article for the paper. She'd developed a close connection with a few residents, which was a two-way street. The residents loved her. Everyone has their own story, and they were drawn to her empathetic nature, like wounded birds who instinctively knew she cared about them. Dr. Gallagher's sessions constantly fueled her empathy and piqued her interest. Today was no exception, as she noticed the attractive brunette across from her once again slumped down in her chair, crying softly.

"Tara, is there anything you'd like to share with the group today?"

Jennifer was as surprised as Dr. Gallagher when Tara looked up and said, "Why doesn't anyone believe me? If they did, I wouldn't be here." Then, she put her head down and visibly zoned out again. Jennifer was surprised Dr. Gallagher didn't encourage her to talk more, but she assumed he knew what he was doing.

<hr/>

"Jennifer, how are you doing? How's that article going?"

"Pretty well." Jennifer was back in Dr. Gallagher's office, and it was liberating to relax and drop her cover behind a closed door with a friend for a change.

"Please don't forget that I need to review your material before publication, in case it involves any doctor-patient confidentiality."

"I completely understand, Tony. I should have some pages for you soon. With Carson out of town for the Atlanta medical conference, I've had more time to concentrate on it. Why haven't you gone? It must be tedious. I haven't been able to reach Carson, unless he's ignoring my calls. Tony, I know you can't tell me anything, but my heart goes out to Tara Montgomery. She is so young and so unhappy."

"Someone has to stay behind to hold down the fort." He didn't have the heart to tell her there was no medical conference in Atlanta. Was Carson up to his old tricks again? He had just seen him in Baton Rouge, walking into Starbucks the night before. "You are absolutely right. I can't, but you can pray for her. She needs all the help she can get."

"Tony, how do you do it?"

"Do what?"

"How do you cope with all the damaged souls you encounter daily, day in and day out? Your patients love you, but it must be exhausting."

"And I love them. When Rene died, I lost my way for a while. She was a sweet soul who never lost faith in God despite everything. I was furious with God for a while. I couldn't rationalize how he could let her suffer that way. I couldn't work for six months; I was a basket case. Eventually, I threw myself back into my work and was grateful for its temporary distraction. At some point, I slowly pulled out of that dark place and noticed a common denominator all my patients shared. Let me put it another way. Before Rene became so ill, she had a fascination with butterflies. We all indulged her. The house was full of butterfly figurines of every color and description. She said they reminded her of the cycle of life and how resilient we all are. Think about it: some of our patients come here from the darkest places, and no matter how damaged they are, like the butterfly, they do everything they can to metamorphose from that dark place and emerge as a new and healthy version of themselves. We all share the resilience of humanity; that emergence is a beautiful thing to see when it happens, and I get to be a part of it. That's why I do it."

Chapter Nine
The Better Man

I don't know what to say, Tony. That is a beautiful analogy; your patients are fortunate to have you as their doctor, and I'm equally proud to have you as my friend."

"Hi, you're new here, aren't you? I've seen you in the hall and at Dr. Gallagher's group sessions. I'm Tara Montgomery. I don't want to bother you; I just wanted to introduce myself and welcome you to Heatherton. Jennifer, isn't it?"

"Of course, I'm glad you did; thank you." I don't know how new I am anymore. I've been here for over four months." This was the first time Jennifer had seen Tara without her crying, so her heart went out to the young girl.

"I was about to go to the dining room for coffee and maybe a muffin. Would you like to join me?"

"Yes, I would. The muffins should be freshly baked by now," she said as they walked down the hall to the dining room. "So, what are you in here for?"

"Nothing too dramatic. I had a stressful job, and it all caught up with me one day: my nerves, my home life, my mother's death, and I had a meltdown. What about you?"

"Hank, my stepfather tried to rape me. When I told my mother, he told her I lied and made the whole thing up, and she believed him. He warned me that he would ensure I never saw her again if I said anything to my mother. One day, when I got home from school, he was already home, and he grabbed me and put his hands all over me. I broke a vase over his head and went to a friend's house for a few days. Hank told my mother I ran away and had me picked up by a truant officer. I told my counselor at school what he did, and she didn't believe me either. I don't know what Hank might have said to convince her I was a juvenile delinquent, or if he knew the truant officer. It was awful. People started looking at me differently in school. One day, Bruce Jackson grabbed me from behind the gym, pinned me against the wall, and started pawing me. "So, you'd rather do it with your old man than someone your age?"

"When I jammed my knee in his groin, he was furious. 'Touch me again, Bruce, and I'll turn you into a girl.' How could anyone know someone so vile even existed?" I was called into the principal's office with my parents and suspended for two weeks for inappropriate behavior on school property and for skipping school. Bruce only received a three-day suspension. My mother never asked me for my version of what happened. My friend's father is a minister, and he told me I needed to give it to the Lord; he would never abandon me. Where is he now? I'm here. God knows the truth, so why is this even happening to me? I don't belong here because they convinced someone I'm crazy and incorrigible. Even the doctors looked at me strangely when I first arrived. Why won't anyone believe me?"

"Oh, Tara, I'm so sorry. I believe you. These individuals who have hurt you gave themselves over to evil long ago. It may seem like they are powerful now, but the worst thing you can do for yourself is to give up on your faith. It would be easy to lose faith in people based on what you've gone through, but remember, you are never defined by what people say about you. You're never a bother to anyone, and you don't have anything to apologize for. Validation starts with you. When you consistently start a sentence with 'I'm sorry,' it reflects the self-image you've developed from the messages you received growing up. When we don't get the support we need from our parents or those we should, we develop unhealthy coping methods and believe we are unworthy. Have you talked to Dr. Gallagher yet? He can help you with this."

"Not yet. I told Ms. Parker a little, but she acted like she didn't believe me and just gave me meds that made me feel funny. I don't feel like myself. When I'm not falling asleep all the time, I'm crying at the slightest provocation. I want my stepfather exposed for the criminal he is and to go to jail, where he can't hurt anyone again. I don't know if I'll ever be able to forgive my mother."

"Tara, you should speak with Dr. Gallagher. I promise you that he will listen to you and be able to help you. Have you considered that you might be precisely where you need to be to get the help you need? We don't always know what God's plan is. It hurts, but you can heal and recover here and start a new life."

…Tara woke up in the middle of the night, drenched in sweat and whimpering. It was a nightmare, but it seemed so real that she thought she was back in her house and her stepfather was pushing against the door, trying to dislodge the chair and get into her room. "I'm done," she said aloud, sitting straight up in bed. Jennifer was right; she would make an appointment with Dr. Gallagher first thing in the morning and expose that pervert and her mother for who they were.

Jennifer woke up to a loud pounding on her door. "Emily, what are you doing at my door at this hour? It's five in the morning."

"I wanted to tell you they just took Tara to the hospital. She tried to commit suicide last night. She was unconscious. She swallowed a whole bunch of pills. The word is she may not make it."

"That's horrible. I thought she was doing so well."

She was, but her mother probably called her. That's what she does, and then Tara relapses. I've got to go before someone finds out I'm not in my room. Pray for her."

There was a dark cloud hanging over Heatherton for days after Tara was rushed to the hospital. It was an invisible cloud, of course, but it was filled with sadness and fear and hovered ominously over all her friends. One of their own was in trouble, and they were worried she wouldn't survive. Jennifer walked into Heatherton's little chapel and was surprised to see many patients praying for Tara. As she sat down, Emily whispered in her ear that Dr. Gallagher had just received a call from the hospital, saying that Tara was out of the ICU and would be all right.

"Tara, I was delighted to hear that you had scheduled an appointment with me. What can I do for you? I'm so glad you're back. You're lucky to be alive, young lady. Would you like to talk about it? Can you tell me what happened? You were doing so well."

"I was Dr. Gallagher until my mother called me that night and started talking about me moving back in whenever I leave here. I told her I would never live there again because of what Hank did. She started screaming at me that I had ruined her life with all my lies. I hung up. It's what she does, but I guess I was at my lowest that night and couldn't throw it off. It seemed the right thing to do at the time: check out and avoid dealing with it. It wasn't a rational solution, but it made sense then. I'm grateful that I failed and for the chance to try again. I think it's time for me, Dr. Gallagher, to take the reins. I am so sick of my parents controlling my life. I've been here for over six months and can't see any improvement. I know I don't always participate in group sessions like I should. You've been so patient with me. I stay in my head so much that I can't focus or sleep, but when I do, I wake up so exhausted that it's as if I never did. I've been talking to Jennifer Nelson, the new girl, and hearing my words coming back to me. It has enabled me to see myself as a marionette being manipulated by my toxic parents and others. I don't want to live like this anymore."

"That's a profound statement, Tara, and a great start. Let's begin there. Can you recall when you first arrived at that conclusion and what might have made you feel that way?"

Once Tara started talking, it was as if someone had let air escape from a balloon. When she finally took a break, she felt a sense of immense relief that was entirely foreign to her, and she liked the feeling. She was surprised at how comfortable she felt sharing feelings with Dr. Gallagher that she had internalized for years, and she was hopeful that, for the first time, she could get through this. Maybe Jennifer was right; she was strong. Dr. Gallagher, what are the eligibility requirements for living in one of the campus cabins at Heatherton? Do you think I ever have a chance of qualifying?"

"Absolutely, we've made a significant breakthrough today, and that's what this program is all about. You are not defined by the things you've gone through with your parents or others. Obtaining a cabin is a final step toward returning to society and resuming your daily life. I have no doubt you would be a good fit. We can complete the paperwork today and get started. How does that sound? It goes before a review board, and given your recent hospital stay, it may be a while before you're approved, but it's a good start. What's the first thing you want to do when you leave Heatherton?"

Chapter Ten
Deception

G o to college. I still have a scholarship. Until I turn eighteen, I am still a minor, and I don't want to ever live with my parents again."

"A simple court order could solve that. You never have to see your parents again. It is your choice. You have several options. As far as that goes, with legal counsel, you could sign yourself out one day if that's what you want. A psychiatrist would have to deem that you were not a threat to anyone or yourself. A judge could assign you a guardian of your choice until you turn eighteen. You can also file a petition with the court to be emancipated. Your parents may have signed you into Heatherton, but that commitment is no longer valid under the circumstances. You might want to consider pressing charges against your stepfather."

"That I can't do soon enough, but I prefer to continue with my therapy and transition out of the program as soon as I'm ready."

"That sounds great, Tara. In the meantime, you can work on completing all the paperwork for that scholarship from here. I'm incredibly proud of you."

"Jack, how are you?"

"Better, I guess. I'm sure you heard I flipped out, and they had to carry me out on a stretcher. Just another reminder that I have no control over my life."

"I'm so sorry, Jack. I can only imagine what you go through on a daily basis. I hope you know how much your service to your country is appreciated."

"Thank you. That means a great deal to me for so many reasons. It was a crazy and senseless war. Dr. Gallagher has devoted a lot of time to me, and I'm sure I am probably making some progress, but it's like Doc says, 'Post Traumatic Stress Disorder (PTSD) is not something you get over, but you have to learn to live with.' I heard you had an anaphylactic reaction to some shellfish. It sounds like we were both carried out of here on a stretcher on the same day. How does an allergic reaction like that ever happen? Shouldn't there have been a red flag on your chart by your nurse?"

"You're right. Edith Parker is my nurse, and I was assured that my shellfish allergy was flagged before I moved in here. I don't know what happened, but she told me it was taken care of."

"Edith Parker, now there's one never to turn your back on."

"What do you mean?"

"First of all, she likes to overmedicate her patients. Maybe she can control them better that way. Who knows? The other thing is she is a bit weird for my taste. I always get the feeling she is hiding something. Everyone here is afraid of her. Let's say I wouldn't want to be on her bad side. I apologize, Jennifer, for my behavior the other day. You were only trying to help. I can't promise I won't be rude on one of my psycho days, but please don't take it personally. Sometimes, the triggers come out of nowhere, and my emotions are like a train wreck. Most of the time, I don't know when they will show up and turn me into a mad dog."

"Apology accepted, Jack. I think I'll turn in for the night. I hear a hot shower and a good book calling me."

Jennifer was grabbing a towel and her robe to take a relaxing shower when she heard a knock at her door." Edith Parker stuck her head in and walked toward her before she had time to open it.

"There you are. I came to check on you." Edith said.

Jennifer couldn't believe Edith's complete disregard for her privacy. It was as if she didn't respect her as a person. Jennifer knew Edith had been apprised of her reason for being at Heatherton by Tony and Carson. Yet she made it a point to condescend to her every time they met as if she were trying to exert some kind of power over her.

"I wanted to let you know that I still don't understand how the kitchen staff overlooked your shellfish allergy. I have notified them of this debacle and assure you that it will never happen again."

"Let's hope not. I could have died. Thank God Dr. Gallagher thought to look in my purse for my EpiPen. When I think of it, I'm surprised that Heatherton's pharmacy doesn't keep Epi-Pens in stock for its patients. I understood that the kitchen was informed of my shellfish allergy before I moved in."

"I'll investigate having Epi-pens aboard and bring them up at our next staff meeting. That is correct. The kitchen was informed; I told them myself. Surely, you are not implying I am responsible for someone else's ignorance."

"I wasn't implying anything of the kind, and I think you know that." Jennifer disliked the woman with a passion, and Edith Parker made no effort to hide her blatant animosity for Jennifer every time she saw her.

⁘⸎⸝⸍⸝⸎⸏⸎

One morning after breakfast, Jennifer noticed some patients were more talkative than usual, even chattering excitedly.

"Emily, what's going on? There's excitement in the air. I've never heard the patients as ramped up as they are this morning."

"It's all about the Sweetheart's Dance. It's a big deal here. The hospital hires a caterer and an excellent band. Many of the patients assist with the decorations. It's only a couple of weeks away. People all dress up in their finest for the event. Heatherton has always been pretty generous with their activities here. I love our Christmas party and Valentine's dance, but this is one of my favorites."

"That is a big deal."

"You must come. Don't let the name fool you. You don't have to have a date. We can go together."

"Okay, that sounds like fun. I'm in."

It was the weekend, and Jennifer met Carson at their house for a night out. Jennifer picked out her best outfit, an emerald green velvet cocktail dress with the back bare to the waist. She took extra time with her hair and makeup. She should have been excited, but her marriage now felt like a farce, and maintaining the pretense was becoming increasingly complex. She had never felt more trapped in her life.

"Jennifer, you've hardly touched your food and seem a thousand miles away." You know how hard it is to get reservations here. You haven't said a word since we left the house. What's going on?"

"Us."

"Us? What now? Am I spending too much time at the office? It's always something with you. Are you ever happy?"

"I'm not one of your patients, Carson. Deflecting isn't going to work with me. We're in trouble, and you know it. I'm undercover in Heatherton, and I've never seen you. It's not like you don't have an office at Heatherton. You completely ignored my calls while you were in Atlanta for your medical conference. When I do see you, you're distracted. I don't think you want to be together anymore. I think it's time we take a break from each other."

"And whose fault is that? It's not like I can see you at Heatherton when you're undercover. It's a two-way street. This was your hare-brained idea, not mine."

"Is there someone else? Are you back to your old habits again?"

"Of course not. You know there's no one else. That's crazy. Why would you even ask me that? Are you ever going to forgive me for one discretion? You sound just like your mother. Are you talking about a divorce?" This is what happens when you hang out with psychotic patients."

"Enough with the gaslighting, Carson. Given your track record, it's not as if you have an immaculate reputation. Drop me off at Heatherton; I'm done."

"Look, honey, I'm sorry. I know I haven't always been the most attentive husband. I promise I'll try to do better. Why don't you save a dance for me at the sweetheart's dance?

"I don't know, Carson. I've had it."

"Fine, I'll take you back to Heatherton then," he said, throwing his napkin down on the table. "That's where you belong, anyway. Don't worry about coming home either." *With her, it's always something. Maybe a divorce would get her off my back, and I could breathe for a change.*

⸻

"Jennifer, I've told you before, you can't believe anything the patients here say to you." Most of them are on heavy medication so that they can cope with their demons, and they can't remember what they had for breakfast, let alone provide an accurate account of anything. Their short-term memory is swimming in a drug cocktail. Consider the source before you nail Carson to the wall. I've known Carson for years, and he's no saint, but this is even a stretch for him."

"You don't believe me, Tony, do you? You see an entirely different Edith Parker than the rest of the world, especially how she treats her patients when no one is looking. Beneath that well-constructed façade she wears, beats a heart of stone. She has disliked me vehemently since the day I met her, for some reason, and doesn't even try to hide it. If Harry believes Edith and Carson are having an affair, he probably saw them together. I have suspected Carson's lack of loyalty to me for years, but never wanted to believe he would cheat on me. It's not like he hasn't gone down that road before. He can charm his way into anything and will look you straight in the face when confronted, until you doubt yourself. I don't see Edith having a strong moral compass either; I wouldn't put anything past her. I've also heard she over-medicates her patients. I know now unequivocally that she was responsible for me going into anaphylactic shock after making sure that I was served a salad with shrimp in it. I'm glad that I finally figured it out. My chart was supposed to indicate that I have a severe shellfish allergy, and the kitchen staff was supposed to be aware of it. There wasn't enough in it to easily discern, or I would have noticed, but she knew how toxic it was for me. By the time I tasted it, it was too late. I could have died, Tony. There was no chance of reporting it, as I'm sure the salad was disposed of before I even arrived at the hospital. Thank God you showed up when you did and thought to look in my purse for an Epi-Pen. You saved my life."

"Yes, you could have. It is a matter of record now with the hospital. I promise I'm not through investigating it, but the allegations you're suggesting are severe and hard to imagine."

Chapter Eleven
The Sweetheart's Dance

Whatever you do, please don't mention this to Carson. We are having some problems of our own right now."

"You should know I wouldn't; there's no need to worry. Just remember, we can shut this down any time you want." His eyes spoke volumes as he quickly looked away, but not before Jennifer saw his raw and exposed feelings blazing across his face.

"I know, Tony, but I still want to do some investigating of my own."

"Just be careful, Jennifer. No newspaper story is worth your life."

"Emily Pettito wasn't kidding. The Sweetheart's Dance was the event of the year. It was staged in a room Jennifer had never seen before, considerably more expansive than the day room or the dining room, and it was buzzing. The decorations were elaborate and festive but not overdone. Residents were dancing in their best clothes. A security guard was on duty. If he was armed, it was well concealed. She wondered if there had ever been an incident challenging the security at Heatherton. Somehow, it made her feel more comfortable knowing he was there. The hospital had picked some fantastic caterers. They had set up an impressive spread, and everyone took full advantage of the delicious food. There was no alcohol served, and no one seemed to mind.

Carson had promised Jennifer he would attend the dance, but she wasn't surprised when he didn't show up. What surprised her the most was how little his absence meant to her, and then she saw Tony walking toward her.

"Jennifer, are you enjoying the Sweetheart's Dance? You look stunning, by the way. I'd love to ask you to dance, but I don't want to blow your cover."

"Yes, I'm impressed. They go all out here, don't they? The food is delicious. Thank you, Tony. I don't want to risk blowing my cover, either."

"You know what, I've changed my mind," he said, reaching for her hand. It is, after all, a dance. Is it my fault you're the most beautiful woman in the room?"

Jennifer knew Tony had feelings for her, even though he never said anything; however, she had never felt that way towards him and chalked it up to his loneliness since Rene's death. She was married, after all. She was utterly unprepared for their chemistry when Tony took her in his arms, and they glided across the dance floor. *He would pick a slow dance,* she thought as she felt his muscular body against hers. *Where were these feelings coming from? Had they always been there? How could she have missed it?* His cologne was like an aphrodisiac.

"Are you about to wrap up your article? I'm looking forward to reading it. Oh, look, here comes Jack Turner. I think he is going to ask you to dance. He looks like he's on a mission, puppy eyes and all. I enjoyed dancing with you."

"Jennifer, would you like to dance?" You look lovely tonight."

"Of course, Jack, I'd love to. Thank you."

"Jennifer, are you okay? Have you had any more allergy episodes? Don't forget what I told you. You can't take your eyes off Edith Parker even for a minute. There is a reason people here are afraid of her. She is unpredictable."

"I won't, Jack, don't worry."

"Can I have this dance with my wife?" Carson asked out of nowhere, rudely pushing Jack aside. "Sorry, buddy."

"Carson, was that necessary? That was rude and uncalled for; you probably have blown my cover.

"Ask me if I care. Who is that old bird anyway? He was practically drooling. Perhaps you'll give up this charade now and come home where you belong.

"Sometimes, Carson, believing you are a psychiatrist is a real challenge. You can be so cruel. You know exactly why I'm here; I still haven't found out what happened to my mother yet. I'm not going anywhere. You figure it out."

Carson glared at her, grabbed her hand, and squeezed it so hard that her eyes watered from the pain, but she wouldn't give him the satisfaction of crying out before he stormed off.

Tony was watching the whole thing and saw Jennifer rubbing her hand. He was furious; it was all he could do not to go after Carson, but he knew Jennifer would be mortified. He pretended not to notice when she walked past him to the restroom. He could see she was crying. He was shocked at what a cad Carson was. It was apparent he'd been drinking a lot. He wasn't the only one who witnessed Carson's temper tantrum. Jack stood next to him and saw the whole thing, clenching and unclenching his fist and imagining how good it would feel to connect with the beast's jaw. "Jack, don't you even think about it," Tony whispered. "He's not worth it."

<hr />

The following day, Jennifer was waiting for the elevator and decided to take the stairs for exercise. She missed her morning runs, and Heatherton's gym fell short of her expectations. One minute, she thought she heard something and sensed someone behind her, and the next thing she knew, she was lying at the bottom of the stairs.

"Jennifer, dear God, are you all right?" Jack asked. What are you doing out here anyway? Don't move; I'm calling an ambulance."

"I think I've broken my ankle. Otherwise, I'm okay. I'll probably have some bruises tomorrow."

"Jennifer, stay right here; hang tight. The ambulance just drove up," Jack said, wrapping an ice pack around her ankle. "I'll let Dr. Gallagher know what happened."

"Mrs. Nelson, your ankle is broken. I am giving you an injection for the pain. That will get you to the hospital until they can set it," the young EMT said.

"Mrs. Nelson, we need to quit meeting like this," Ben, the young nurse from her last visit, said. "I hear you fell down some stairs. Let's get you into X-ray and see how much damage you've done this time. You'll probably feel like you've been hit by a Mack truck tomorrow."

"Tony, what are you doing here?"

"Jennifer, I just heard. I got here as soon as I could. What happened? Jack Hale told me you fell down the stairs."

"It looks worse than it is. I broke my ankle in two places and only had a few bruises. Tony, can you give me a ride back to Heatherton? I didn't fall; I was pushed. I'm quite sure it was Edith."

"You can't be serious. If you're right, you need to shut everything down and get out of Heatherton, whoever it was. What in the world would make you think it was Edith?"

"I know what Shalimar smells like. That's her perfume. I heard someone behind me as I was walking down the stairs, but she pushed me before I could turn around. She would have had to step over me to leave, as the panic bar locked automatically when we went through it, and she would have exited through the door. I'm sure I saw a flash of her blond hair when she stepped over me just before I passed out. She left me there to die. I'm not leaving until I find out what happened to my mother. Maybe Edith is behind the whole thing."

"Hang in there, and I'll get your discharge papers and bring them to you if they'll even let you check out." We'll finish discussing this in the car.

"Okay, Jennifer, they're letting you leave. You'll be on bed rest for two days and use crutches until the cast is removed. Here comes the wheelchair. I'll go and get the car and meet you outside at the front door."

Tony confiscated a pillow and another ice pack from the emergency room nurse and propped Jennifer's foot up when he helped her into the car. "I know you must be in a lot of pain, but does that help at all? I still don't know how you didn't break your neck. What were you doing on the stairs anyway? If Jack hadn't found you, I shudder to think how long you might have lain there."

"It helps a lot, thank you. I'm sure God sent his team of angels because I was halfway down the stairs before I was pushed. You know how slow the elevators are. I thought the exercise would do me good, so I was clipping along and had already gone halfway down when Edith caught up with me. I imagine she'll be livid when she realizes I'm still alive. By the way, I told Carson we needed to separate for a while. What a week."

"Jen, how do you think you'll survive now? You're on crutches, for heaven's sake."

"I know, but I can't think about that right now. My head hurts too much."

"I'll send Alford to your room to install a deadbolt on your door in case she tries again. Please use it every time you're in your room. Do you think she knows you saw her? What about Carson?"

"What about Carson? God only knows what lies he'll come up with this time for not showing up at the hospital. I'm done."

Chapter Twelve
More Betrayal

ay to go, Tony." It was after hours, and all he wanted to do was go home, shower, and fall asleep. Tony was almost at the front door when he realized he had forgotten his phone in his office. As he passed Carson's office, he thought he heard something and simultaneously realized the door was slightly open. *What the Hell!* About to barge in, he saw Carson and Edith Parker through the opening, ripping their clothes off. They must have been in such a hurry that they forgot to close the door behind them. He was positive they didn't hear or see him walk away. *Jennifer was right, after all. He knew Carson was full of himself and thought the world owed him something, but this was unconscionable. Jennifer didn't deserve this. This put a whole different slant on everything. Could Edith be sabotaging Jennifer's every move? Was she indeed responsible for ensuring Jennifer was served shrimp in her salad?* He had to let her know she was in danger. *Was Carson in on it, too? What was in it for him besides his obvious lust for women? He didn't seem to care much if he got caught.*

"Jennifer, you need to wrap up this outrageous idea of yours. You are in imminent danger. Your life isn't worth a news article; your boss probably wouldn't even read or appreciate it. Didn't you hear me say that I saw Carson and Edith going at it last night in his office? They were so much into each other; they forgot to close the door all the way."

"I did hear you. That sure explains why Edith despises me, doesn't it? Tony, you don't understand; that is only part of the story. I'm here to research for a feature story on Heatherton, but I'm also here to find out who murdered my mother. I think Edith had something to do with it, and now she is trying to stop me from finding out what happened. Now she's even tried to kill me for the second time. Too many things don't add up, and they haven't from the beginning."

"I believe what you're saying about Edith having it in for you. Perhaps it's more than a fling for her; she wants Carson for herself. Lord knows they deserve each other, but murder? That's why you asked me about Dr. Denton, isn't it? Do you honestly think he had anything to do with whatever happened to your mother? Surely, you realize if he sees you here or you approach him to ask questions, it will most certainly blow your cover." Suddenly, he grabbed her by her shoulders. "Jennifer, you could be in grave danger, and I'm concerned that you're not taking this seriously and are still insisting on staying here. I'm worried about you. There's no way you can continue to stay here now." Suddenly, he let his feelings take over, pulled her into his arms, and kissed her passionately. To her surprise, Jennifer responded to his embrace and kissed him back with all the feelings she had been trying to ignore."

"Tony, this is a mistake. I'm still married, regardless," she said, pushing him away.

"I know you're right. I'm sorry, we can't lose our heads now. I had no idea you thought your mother was murdered here. I'm sure you have something to support your suspicions.

"Yes, I do. Ironically, I'm about done with my article. I think I will go back to my room for a bit and lie down. I need to process all this information. I knew I couldn't trust Carson for years, but he was adept at avoiding detection; I thought he had changed. Getting confirmation like this has confirmed what a fool I've been and is forcing me to face the truth."

"Jennifer, I'm so sorry about everything."

"Don't be. I needed to know. When the dust settles, it might be a relief. Years ago, I gave him an ultimatum and wanted to believe he had changed, but I guess I wasn't ready to accept he had no intention of changing. I've been such a fool. He was supposedly always attending those meetings and medical conferences. No one is as blind as those who don't want to see."

"Jennifer, please don't malign yourself like that."

"I'll try. Tony, someone here told me there's a morgue in the basement."

"There is, but surely you aren't considering checking it out, are you? That's insane."

"Yes, I am. It looks like I've stirred up a hornet's nest, and I don't know how long I will have before someone tries to stop me again and maybe succeed this time. I want to see if I can check the computer files to see what they say about the day my mother died. Maybe that will bring something up. Is there any way I could access them?"

"My God, you're serious. Jennifer, this is crazy. You're still hobbling around on a cast, for heaven's sake. The morgue has an entirely different antiquated system and has never been synced with ours. I think it will be upgraded eventually, but I haven't heard anything this year yet. There is no way. You must present an ID card to enter the premises and access the password-protected computer files. I don't even know the password. There might be some backup paper files, but I'm not even sure if they are current or filed correctly.

Jennifer knew she would jeopardize Tony's job if she asked him to borrow his ID card, and she didn't want to put him on the spot by even asking. She would figure it out somehow. She couldn't sleep that night. Her mind kept racing back and forth whenever she closed her eyes. She decided to get up and remembered that Tony had mentioned the laundry earlier. She found it close to the dining room, just as Tony said. She couldn't believe her good luck. Someone must have forgotten to lock it. It didn't take her long to find what she was looking for. She had noticed the nurses wore one color of scrubs and the doctors another. She discovered some scrubs in her size hanging up on a large rack, probably ready to be picked up soon. Now, she had to figure out what to do with her clothes. She changed into a pair of light blue scrubs and stuffed the sweatpants and shirt she'd been wearing into a plastic bag she spotted on a shelf and into an empty laundry bin. She stuck her head out the door, looked both ways, and made a beeline for the elevator. When the elevator doors opened in the basement, she could see the brilliant glare of fluorescent lights under a door she assumed was the morgue, less than thirty feet ahead of her, and the door was ajar. Perspiration was running down the back of her neck. *Tony was right. This was insane. She needed her head examined.*

"Hello, where did you come from? This is an unauthorized area, you know. I don't see any ID. How did you get in here, anyway?"

"Hey, big boy, you startled me. The door wasn't closed all the way. Are you here all by yourself? It's spooky down here. I'm Cassandra Trent. My friends call me Cassie. I've only been working here a week," she said, winking at him. "Would you believe I forgot it?" You wouldn't want to help a girl in a cast out, would you? It wouldn't look too good for me to get written up my first week now, would it?" she said, looking up at him seductively and picking an imaginary piece of lint off his collar.

"What are you doing here?" he asked, his gaze sweeping over her. "This is a morgue; there are only dead people here, and no nurses are needed. How did you get the cast anyway?"

"It's hardly worth mentioning. I'm a clutz; what can I say? I'm doing a favor for a friend. She thought she had made an error in someone's file, and I told her I'd check for her. She couldn't come herself because she was afraid someone would catch her. On the other hand, I haven't been here long enough for anyone to recognize me. It's the least I can do; she's been a big help since I arrived. She took me under her wing, so I felt obligated to return the favor."

"Okay, but you owe me big," he said, looking her up and down again and stopping at her chest. "Come on, I'm on the computer, so you'll have to look at the hard copies. There's the file cabinet. When did the patient pass away? We have an outdated system down here, which is actually archaic and will soon be upgraded, thank goodness. I'm Mark Cannon, by the way. My shift is almost over, so make it quick. I'm taking a significant risk. I could lose my job, you know, and I have rent and a car payment to pay, so please do it quickly. It's unlikely, but if someone does come in, there's a bathroom in that corner; I'd advise you to make a run for it, and I never saw you. You're on your own if you get busted."

"Got it, handsome." *I hope I find what I need and make it out of here in one piece.* Despite the fluorescent lights, it was all Jennifer could do to make herself stay. The dank air smelled of death and formaldehyde. The absence of windows made Jennifer feel claustrophobic, causing the hair on the back of her neck to stand up.

Mark returned to his ancient metal desk, which looked like it had seen better days, and turned his back to her. He sat down at the computer and started typing.

It was beginning to look like someone forgot to include the hospital morgue in the budget. All the office equipment looked like it came from a salvage store. It was a risky move, but it was the best she could think of. Her heart was beating so fast she could hear it in her ears. She was way over her head and hoped this creep didn't grab her in the hall when she was ready to leave. Mark had unlocked the file cabinet for her, but when she pulled out the top drawer, it creaked and groaned like it hadn't been opened in years. She had to turn her back on Mark and was terrified the whole time that he might come up behind her. Tony was right. What on earth could she have been thinking? Fortunately, the files were well organized, and it became apparent in short order that there was no information on the day her mother died; in fact, there was no file at all showing her mother was ever a patient at Heatherton or even existed. "Okay, handsome, I'm done. Got to go."

"Wait a minute. My shift is over in five minutes. Do you want to go somewhere to eat? I'm starving."

"No, I'm sorry, Mark; I'm working a double shift tonight." I barely have enough time to shower and come back. I'll probably have to shower here at the hospital. Thank you so much for your help. Maybe another time," she said, hurrying past him as quickly as she could, ignoring his red face. When she reached the elevator, she realized she'd been holding her breath, expecting him to show up and grab her at any minute. When she got off the elevator, she was shaking like a leaf. She hurried to the laundry room, grabbed the plastic bag containing her sweats from the laundry bin, and made it to her room without being seen. She shed the scrub pants, dropped them on the bathroom floor, made a mad dash to the bedroom, dove under the covers, and was asleep the minute her head hit the pillow. The next morning, Jennifer was horrified; she had forgotten to set her alarm and overslept. Great, *I've missed breakfast; it looks like vending machines for me this morning.* As she bent over to pick up the scrubs she had dropped on the bathroom floor the night before and walked back into the bedroom, she realized she was staring directly at the plant by the accent chair; the light coming through the window had caught something, making her look. "You've got to be kidding me, a camera?"

Chapter Thirteen
Mark Cannon

Jennifer, I've been so worried. I thought you'd have called me by now. What did you find out?"

"I'm sorry, Tony, I overslept this morning. I didn't even make it for breakfast. I couldn't get out of my head last night and fall asleep, so I went to the basement and met Mark Cannon. As creepy as he was, I convinced him it was my first week as a charge nurse, and I had to access the filing cabinet to check a file for a friend who had made an entry error. There was no record of my mother ever having been here, nor was there any information from the coroner."

"That is crazy. I knew you'd do it, but I'm glad I didn't know when. Mark Cannon is a creepy guy, and there's no telling what he might be capable of. I'm glad you brought an army of angels with you."

"It proves what I've said all along; someone has gone to an awful lot of trouble to destroy any information that would help me find out what happened to my mother. What about Dr. Denton? Did someone destroy his notes, or were there ever any in the first place? That is probably why I got the threatening note I did. Whoever killed my mother is getting uncomfortable. I must be getting too close."

"What threatening note?"

When I got up this morning, I found someone had slipped a note under my door sometime during the night. I'm sure it wasn't there before I went to bed."

"What did it say?"

"Keep sticking your nose where it doesn't belong, and you will suffer the consequences."

"Jennifer, that's insane. Hang onto it. You've got to go to the police before something happens to you."

"That's not all," she said, handing Tony a tiny camera. I found this in a plant in my room," she said. "I'm furious. My artwork for the Times-Picayune article is also gone. Obviously, someone has been in my room; I have no idea how many times. That freaks me out."

"Jennifer, this is serious. What are you going to do? What are you waiting for, until someone murders you in your bed? Aren't you using the deadbolt I installed on your door?"

"I'm sure the camera was installed in my room long before you ever put a deadbolt on my door, probably right after I moved in. I would never have seen it if a light reflection hadn't caught my eye. I promise to contact the police as soon as I can gather enough evidence. I'm close. They wouldn't give me the time of day now, you know that. I don't understand why someone planted a camera. As for my article, I had already forwarded my artwork to Pete, so I'm safe there. It makes my skin crawl to think that someone has been going through my things. I feel violated. What gives them the right to invade my privacy like this?"

The following day, as soon as Jennifer walked into the dining room, she saw Mark Cannon, the employee from the morgue, sitting at a table across the room. At the same time, Emily called out to her. "Jennifer, come sit with me." She couldn't do anything but sit down with Emily at the risk of making a scene if she left. Emily's voice carried across the entire dining room like a foghorn. Jennifer was sure Mark had noticed her, but she tried to relax as Emily's voice faded into the chaotic background of her thoughts."

Not only had Mark noticed Jennifer, but he was seething. *Who does she think she is? She's just like my mother.* Mark Cannon grew up as a lonely child. His mother never wanted children and didn't care who knew it. The only way he could get her attention was to act out by breaking something or making a mess. She couldn't even be bothered to discipline him. "What did I ever do to deserve a child like you?" she would say. "Let your father handle this. He's the one who wanted a son, not me."

⋆⋆⋆⋆⋆⋆⋆

"Jennifer, you haven't heard a word I've said. Where are you this morning? I need to go; I have an appointment with Dr. Gallagher. I don't want to be late."

"I'm sorry, Emily. You're right; my mind is all over the place."

"It's okay. I'll see you at lunch, and we can catch up. Don't look now, but that dude over there is staring at you. He looks creepy, and he appears to be upset about something. Do you need me to stay? I know some karate."

"No, go on. I'm just leaving anyway." Before Jennifer could get up and head for the door, Mark Cannon was at her table, looking down at her. Apparently, his size didn't slow him down.

"Cassie, right? You're certainly a hard lady to find. You took off pretty fast the other night. I see you no longer have your cast. That's some walk you have. A man could lose his mind. I wanted to take you out to dinner. You hurt my feelings. You owe me, after all. I stuck my neck out for you and then you ran off."

"I'm so sorry, Mark. Today is my day off. I have a couple of things I need to enter on the computer, and then I'm gone. I was grabbing something to eat before I got started. Another time, maybe," she said, heading for the door. She could feel Mark looking at her as she exhaled. *That was a little too close for me. Oh, here comes Tony, my hero.*

"Jennifer, where are you going in such a hurry? Is everything okay? You look like you saw a ghost."

"A ghost would be easier to deal with," she whispered, looking over her shoulder. Tony, I'm sorry, I'm on my way to the library to turn in a book. Can I catch you later?"

<hr />

"Jennifer, I thought that was you. What a pleasant surprise. It has been a while. Do you have someone staying here at Heatherton?"

"Dr. Denton, so nice to see you again. I do, in fact, have an old college friend who lives here. It has been a while, hasn't it?"

"You are looking well. I was so shocked when your mother passed away so suddenly. Your mother had dementia, but otherwise, she was extremely healthy. My wife and I had gone to our cabin in Montana for a week. No emails or cell connection; we never even used our landline. It was wonderful. When I got back, she had already died and been cremated, and I had to refer to Dr. Aten, who was on duty that night, for my notes to close her file. I couldn't believe I was never notified. I made sure my cabin's number was available. She was my patient."

Jennifer struggled to appear as natural as she could despite the rapid beating of her heart. *If Dr. Denton wasn't even at Heatherton when her mother died, then who was responsible? Dr. Aten?* She was so confused. "Dr. Denton, it was great to see you again. I'm afraid I'm running late for an appointment in town and need to go."

Dr. Denton was a handsome man with thick salt-and-pepper hair and brown eyes. His six-foot-four countenance added to his distinguished image and flawless reputation. His place in the world was well-deserved, and he was respected by his colleagues and patients alike. For the moment, he was perplexed, and his furrowed forehead reflected his confusion. He intuited that there was more to Jennifer's conversation than what appeared but had no idea what.

"Tony, have you got a minute? I hate to call you without any warning."

"What's going on? Are you okay?"

"I just ran into Dr. Denton."

"Oh no, did you blow your cover?"

"No, I don't think so. I told him I was visiting an old college friend. He told me he was shocked to find out my mother had died. He and his wife were on vacation, and when he got back, she had already been cremated. He said that, except for dementia, she was in excellent health. I don't think he has a clue, and no one had even notified him the whole time he was gone. That leaves Dr. Aten, who was the doctor on duty the night my mom supposedly died. Dr. Denton said he had to refer to Dr. Aten's notes to close her file, so what happened to the file?"

"That doesn't surprise me about Dr. Denton. Brent is an excellent doctor with an unequaled ethical reputation. I know you must be more confused than ever, though. Dr. Aten isn't here anymore. He works at Lady of the Lake in Baton Rouge. I have a group meeting downstairs in ten minutes. Can I call you tonight?"

"Sure, talk to you later."

That afternoon, Tony made a call to Lady of the Lake. "Dr. Aten, please."

Dr. Aten is no longer with us. Can I help you with anything else?"

Tony Gallagher was back in his office pulling an all-nighter, but when he started nodding off at his computer, he decided it wasn't worth it and started packing up.

Suddenly, he realized he had never called Jennifer back and couldn't resist going by her room to check on her before he left. He knocked lightly and slowly tried her door. *Why hadn't she used the deadbolt, for heaven's sake?* She was sound asleep on her back, her beautiful auburn hair spread out on the pillow. He felt a stab of guilt when he saw her sleeping. She was so lovely. He knew he had fallen hopelessly in love with her and had no right to hope, as her life was in such a mess. He slipped quietly out of her room. Sometimes, he thought she might have feelings for him, too, but nothing had been mentioned since they kissed the other night, and she had made it clear she wasn't interested in going down that road. Carson didn't deserve her. He managed to scrounge a cup of typical bitter and stale hospital coffee from one of the vending machines on the way to his office to pick up his briefcase, only to hear Carson talking to someone in his office. Initially, he thought Carson was on the phone until he heard a woman's voice answer. He didn't knock this time and did a double-take when he opened the door. A woman was sitting on Carson's desk, and Carson was unbuttoning her blouse with his back to the door. *It couldn't be.* Were his eyes playing tricks on him? Tony would have thought he was looking at Jennifer if he hadn't just seen her asleep in her room. It was uncanny, but they were identical, except that the woman Carson was undressing was not Jennifer; she looked exactly like her, and now she was looking directly at him.

"Well, Tony, didn't your mother tell you to knock first before you enter a room? Put your teeth back in your mouth. As you can see, Jennifer and I came into my office for privacy. Unless watching is your thing, be a prince, turn around, and leave. You're a big boy. Whatever it is, it can wait until tomorrow."

"No, it can't, you pig. I just saw Jennifer less than five minutes ago. Does she know you are doing her sister now? First, Edith Parker, and now this woman. You're pathetic. You don't deserve a woman like Jennifer."

"Spare me your holier-than-thou condemnation, Tony. You're just jealous because we both know you've wanted Jennifer for yourself for years."

"I now know that you and Edith have conspired and colluded since Jennifer's first day she arrived for her research. How smug you must have felt when Edith and her sister played right into your hands. Is it Jennifer's money you are after? Too many bad investments and trying to impress your squeeze of the month? Did you plan to kill Jennifer and then marry her sister, and the two of you could live happily ever after, spending her money?" It was apparent the woman sitting on the desk knew nothing about Edith, as she surprised Tony and Carson both with a loud slap across his arrogant face, hastily buttoned up her blouse, jumped down from the desk, and headed for the door, running into Tony on her way out.

"Tiffany, baby, wait, I can explain."

Just like when we were in college. You never could think with your brain. This time, it has caught up with you. Now, what are you going to do? Did you kill their mother, you cad?"

Tony turned and was reaching for the doorknob when suddenly he was hit on the back of the head with something. Everything went black, and the floor rushed up to meet him.

Chapter Fourteen
Surprise! Surprise! Surprise!

Harry, what are you doing in my room? You know, you could get into a lot of trouble for this." Jennifer noticed that she had forgotten to engage the deadbolt again.

"I know, Jennifer, but you are the only one who believes me and doesn't think I'm nuts."

"How did you get back in this ward anyway?"

"I can't blow his cover; I can only say that Jack has figured out how to break the keypad codes. He's a genius. I couldn't sleep as usual and was wandering around. I heard someone beating on the door from inside the supply closet. I tried the door, but it was locked. I heard moaning, all muffled like. I went to Dr. Gallagher's office to tell him. The door was unlocked, wide open, and it looked like a tornado had hit it. Papers were scattered everywhere. The file cabinet drawers were still open, as if someone had been looking for something and left in a hurry. What if Dr. Gallagher is in trouble? Come on, we have to get Jack. I think he told me once he knew how to pick locks. He's my buddy, and he gets me. I've never shared this with anyone, not even Dr. Gallagher, but I come from a family of third-generation war heroes. I always planned to be the fourth, but they wouldn't take me because I have a heart murmur. I tried all the service branches but still got the same result. My parents said it didn't matter, but every time my father looked at me, I could see the disappointment in his eyes. Jack looked at me and saw who I really was from the first time we met. He made me finally realize it didn't matter. Come on, Hurry! We need Jack. Dr Gallagher needs us; I can feel it."

"They were in Jack's room, and Harry held a broom he had confiscated somewhere for protection over Jack's bed. Stand back, Jennifer! This dude is liable to wake up like Muhammad Ali, and I can't afford to have him mess up this face. What would the ladies say?" Jack woke up and grabbed the broom handle so quickly that Harry lost his balance and fell backward. He popped up and was at the door before he could ever hit the floor.

"Hey Jack, it's cool. We mean no harm to you. We need your help. Dr. Gallagher might be in big trouble. Do you remember how to pick locks?" Jack threw back the covers, was on his feet in seconds, and was fully dressed in camouflage fatigues, except for the slippers he stepped into beside his bed.

"Lead the way," he said, joining Harry at the door.

"Uh, oh. Hide, guys."

"What's going on here?"

"Hey man, I'm glad to see you," Harry said, tapping the hospital's burly security guard on the shoulder. The toilet in the men's bathroom is clogged, and the entire bathroom is flooded. What a disgusting mess. I almost lost my dinner." The minute the security guard ran back to his station to radio for a plumber, Harry motioned for Jack and Jennifer to come out from hiding and follow him. By the time they had maneuvered themselves through the dimly lit hall, Jack had cracked two ward keycodes and was finally able to get to the supply closet; Jack had done his magic and picked the lock. When they opened the door, a furious, tied, and gagged Dr. Gallagher fell out and tumbled at their feet.

"Holy cow, this is just like Law and Order," Harry said. "I love it." As soon as Jack pulled Tony's gag out, he said. "Harry, call the police." Jennifer was in shock and froze in place. Jack untied him in seconds, and Tony took Jennifer to a nearby lounge while they waited for the police.

As the police left, Tony said, "Jennifer, let's go into my office. You need to sit down for this. When they pick Carson up, it won't matter if he sings like a bird or not. He told me plenty before he knocked me out, tied me up, and threw me in the supply closet. I think he saw me as a liability and intended to come back and kill me later. When they finish charging him for everything — extortion, collusion with Edith Parker, and with your sister —the three of them are in for a shock. If your sister doesn't kill Edith first, she has some serious explaining to do. I never realized you had an identical twin. Why didn't I know this?"

"I'm sorry, it's complicated. We haven't spoken for over two years since she stole thousands from my mother years ago when she was supposed to be taking care of her. That's when my mother moved in with us. It still hurts to talk about. How did you know I was a twin, and who are they?"

"I didn't. I was working late and packing up to leave, so I decided to go and check on you. I might add that you were safe in your bed, sound asleep, without the deadbolt engaged. I was able to walk right in. When I returned to my office to retrieve my briefcase, I heard Carson talking in his office. I assumed he was on the phone until I heard a woman's voice. When I opened the door, I thought I was seeing things. Imagine my surprise when I see a woman, an identical copy of you, sitting on Carson's desk, and he is undressing her. I would have thought it was you if I hadn't just visited your room to check on you. The cad told me it was you and chastised me for barging in on them. Can you believe it? Everything you told me was running through my mind. That husband of yours gets around. I can't wrap my mind around how he can look at himself in the mirror. The man has no moral compass whatsoever. Are you okay? I know this is a lot to absorb, but please brace yourself. There's more. I'll get you a glass of water."

When Carson returned with a glass of water, Jennifer looked pale and exhausted.

"What about my mother? Did Edith kill her, or was it Carson?"

"Edith did not kill your mother. Neither Carson nor Tiffany did. Your mother is alive."

"My mother is alive?" Jennifer burst into tears, overwhelmed with relief. "How is that even possible?" Her brain struggled to process. She began to shake and stare ahead as if in a daze.

Tony took her by her shoulders. "Jennifer, I promise you, your mother is alive. They were talking about your mother when I approached the door. I don't have all the details yet, but your sister has been living with your mother somewhere and caring for her. Maybe your friend Emily is right. Maybe the drug cocktail your sister or Edith has been giving her has been the source of her confusion and disorientation. Maybe Edith and your husband were behind this whole thing, getting her diagnosed with dementia, etc. Ironically, neither of the women was aware of the other's involvement with Carson until now. He used them both. I'm sure more will come out when the police pick up the three of them."

I still can't believe my mother is alive. I guess that explains why there are no records in the morgue. What about Dr. Denton and Dr. Aten? Were they also involved? How could they not be? Someone destroyed her file. I wonder who the poor soul was they cremated."

"That was probably the easiest of all to accomplish. The morgue is always an excellent source for homeless cadavers, and no one would be the wiser if a Jane Doe homeless person came up missing. Forging papers is also a no-brainer if you know what you're doing. I don't know about Dr. Denton. Don't forget, he was in Montana when your mother supposedly died and was clueless, so I think it's conclusive that Carson, Edith, and your sister are responsible. I'm so sorry, Jen. How are you taking all this?"

If you mean Carson, I'm not shocked, but my sister—I can hardly believe it. Finding out my mother is alive is surreal. I can barely wrap my mind around it."

"As soon as I hear back from the police and we know where your mother is, let's plan to pick her up. While we wait to hear from them, we need to get you checked out of here and find you and your mother somewhere to stay until we're sure Carson is in jail. He could come after you. We still don't know who put that note under your door."

"It was probably Carson. He's always had a flair for the dramatic. Once they are all in custody, I'll be fine."

Tony didn't share her sentiments but kept his fears to himself.

<hr>

"Well, if it isn't the little nurse from the second floor. Ready to honor your promise to go to dinner with me and have some fun?

"Oh, Mark, it seems like I have other plans every time I see you. I'm sorry."

"Look, you little tease." Before Jennifer had time to react, Mark grabbed her by both shoulders and pinned her to the wall in a dark corner, covering her face with his stale cigarette breath.

"You've got two seconds to get out of my face, you creep, or I'll scream loud enough to bring down the house. I just saw Dr. Gallagher not even a minute ago."

"I did, too, and he's long gone for the day. Don't you dare get high and mighty with me. I'm well acquainted with your type," he said, tightening his grip on her arms. "I did some checking, and there is no Cassandra Trent who works here; there never has been. You're probably not even a nurse. Where are your scrubs or ID? You're lucky I haven't reported you yet. On the other hand, I might be persuaded under certain circumstances to change my mind," he said, whispering in her ear.

"What's going on here? This better not be what it looks like, Mark Cannon, or we might have a fundamental problem," Tony said, holding Mark up by the back of his shirt. "Are we clear? Don't forget, I have your ID number."

"Yes, very clear, Dr. Gallagher. There's no problem," he said, pulling loose from Tony's grip and practically sprinting down the hall.

"Jen, are you okay? I should have pulverized that pervert while I had the chance. Come on, let's go back to my office. You're shaking. That little performance sealed his fate; Mark Cannon will not work another day at Heatherton. I will be making a report to personnel today. I know his supervisor as well. I don't think he'll bother you again, but if he does, I want to hear about it. Sit down, he said, putting a cup of steaming hot coffee in her hands. "Drink up; it's a fresh pot. Jennifer, I was coming to tell you that I just got off the phone with Officer Britton. Do you want to go to lunch? I can tell you what Officer Britton said on the way."

J ennifer hardly said a word in the car on their way to the diner."

"How are you? Did you get any rest at all last night?"

"Not really. I can't believe we went to Mother's memorial service and everything. What was Carson's reason for faking her death in the first place?"

"It seems your sister wouldn't hear of anything else. With your mom presumed dead, all they had to worry about was you. Your sister secured power of attorney over your mother, steadily siphoning off her money. They have been in Ok City for two years, since they faked her death, and no one knew Tiffany had a twin. After all, you both have the same DNA. How would it ever come up?" Your mom wasn't a capable communicator. I guess that explains all of Carson's bogus conferences and meetings. Since Carson failed through Edith to kill you, his backup plan was to have you declared insane and then have you committed. I'm not sure how they planned to pull that off. Whenever your mother passed away, Tiffany would inherit, as you would be lost in the system, and they could live happily ever after with your mother's money. Maybe Emily was right. Your mother is in a hospital in Oklahoma City as we speak, being evaluated. When they picked up Tiffany, she requested that they take your mother by ambulance to Integris Baptist Medical Center. It's beginning to look like your sister used drugs to get your mother interdicted so she could get a power of attorney. What's to say that she needed to maintain your mother's incompetence so she could maintain total control over your mother's money until she passed away of natural causes, unless Carson could have come up with something sooner that wouldn't show up in an autopsy? They have both been arrested and are awaiting arraignment. Edith has also been picked up. Your suspicions were valid; Edith got Dr. Aten to help destroy any paper trail of your mother ever having been here. It must have been right after Dr. Denton got back from his vacation, and Dr. Aten satisfied Dr. Denton's questions with his fabricated notes. There's no telling how Edith managed to get him to help her. It's interesting how he double-crossed her and headed for the hills, yet she remains here. She sang like a bird when she realized he was gone. They'll catch him eventually. Perhaps you should stay in a hotel until you know if Carson will be granted bail. As soon as Carson was arrested, he immediately tried to get immunity by pointing a finger at Edith and your sister, but it backfired. When Tiffany heard that Carson had been seeing Edith Parker the other night, his money scheme died a quick death. Just give me the word, and we'll grab a flight to visit your mother in Oklahoma City."

"I'm ready and can't wait to see her. I still can't believe what my sister did, but I refuse to let it derail me. I know I should see her; I have so many questions, but how could I believe anything she would tell me? I don't know if I ever will."

"I get it. Perhaps you can focus on seeing your mom right now and address confronting your sister later.

When Jennifer and Tony's plane landed in Oklahoma City, she was oblivious to the heat waves rising from the tarmac and everything around her. She felt like she was in a daze when they entered the rental car. It was all so surreal. Her mother was alive. *Why was she so numb? Why wasn't she beside herself with excitement? Was she still in shock?*

Tony was so gentle. He helped her into the cab and took her hand as they exited the vehicle. When they finally arrived at Integris Baptist Medical Center's massive campus, he held her hand, led her to a chair in the beautiful waiting room, and took off momentarily. She barely noticed. When he returned, he had two coffees and a huge grin on his face. "So, are we ready?"

When Tony led her down a long hall, and they walked into room 119, Jennifer gasped. Her mother was sitting up in bed, completely alert and looking as healthy as she had been many years ago.

"Jennifer, darling, come give your mother a hug." Let me look at you, my beautiful daughter. I can't believe it."

"Mom, I can't believe you're alive. I love you so much," she said, touching her mother's face and collapsing into her arms. Her mother's eyes were bright with tears, and she was taking in every detail of her daughter's face as if they had been apart for years, and indeed, they had. Thanks to the drug cocktail her mother had been on for two years and the lie that she had died, Jennifer never had a clue. Jennifer didn't know how much her mother knew yet about what she had suffered at the hands of Tiffany and Edith. She knew she would never let her mother out of sight again until she was sure she was safe. She still hadn't had time to process the betrayal Edith, Tiffany, and Carson had managed to pull off right under her nose. The sheer magnitude of it left her mind reeling. How could she have lived with Carson, slept in their bed, and never known who he was? Edith Parker had tried to kill her twice and managed to find time to sleep with Carter, too. She thanked God she was still alive and had discovered the truth in time.

"Jennifer, have you seen your sister since discovering all this?"

Jennifer jumped, her thoughts scattering as she was unsure how much her mom knew and what she should say.

"Dr. Winters filled me in on everything; Carson's cheating only confirmed what I have suspected for years, I'm afraid. The rest of it is incomprehensible."

"I'm so sorry, Mom; I don't know if I ever want to see Tiffany again. She drugged you, Mom, and stole your money. She was sleeping with Carson."

"I know, honey. I'm so glad your father never lived to see all this, but Edith is the one who put me on all that medicine before they came and got me. I don't think Tiffany ever doubted I had dementia. It's all a bit hazy to me, but I do remember letting Edith think I had taken my meds sometimes, and then I'd feel better. She must have caught on, though, because she stood over me and checked every time I took the pills to make sure I had swallowed them. Most of it is still a blur, though. I'm afraid I was in such a drugged stupor that I couldn't defend myself. It hurts that my own daughter could be a part of something so heinous. I can barely wrap my mind around any of it. It's no excuse, but your sister has always been weak and vulnerable where men were concerned, and Carson took advantage of her. Sometimes, I heard her crying at night. Can you imagine how she felt when she found out Carson was sleeping with Edith?

"No, I can't, Mom, but I don't care right now. She was sleeping with my husband. Sounds a little like poetic justice. I am still so angry. They're all in jail, waiting to be arraigned. It's a nightmare. As soon as Dr. Winters releases you, I would like you to come and live with me. It's only temporary until I can find another place to live. I won't stay in that house a minute longer than I have to. You are welcome to stay with me as long as you like."

"I'd like that until I can regain my strength, and then perhaps you can help me find a place of my own to live."

They talked for hours, making plans and trying to catch up.

"Ms. Nelson, I can no longer turn the other way. Visiting hours were over hours ago," The nurse said. "Your mother will be here tomorrow."

Tony drove Jennifer back to the hotel, but neither said much. Tony was worried about how she would manage the whole debacle. Jennifer was a strong woman, but he worried about how she would process everything. Finding her mother alive and well was one thing, but discovering the treachery behind it was enough to derail anyone.

<hr/>

"Hey guys, what's going on? Come in. What brings you here to my part of the woods?"

"We heard you had moved to one of the 'cabins,' and we wanted to check it out. This is nice," Jack said. "How do you like it?"

"What did you have to do to get one?" Harry asked. "This is cool. I think the cabins are a real plus here. It gives you time to ready yourself to return to the real world again. Ingenious."

I spoke with Dr. Gallagher, and he said I was ready. Considering the circumstances, I put my name on a waiting list, and one became available relatively soon. Dr. Gallagher says they are in high demand, so I'm convinced it was divine intervention that I was able to get one, especially after my botched suicide attempt. I'm excited and transitioning out in a couple of weeks."

"That's amazing, Tara. I'm so happy for you, but we'll miss you."

"Yes, we will," Harry said. "Promise you'll keep in touch with us so we can come and see you."

"I will, I promise."

<hr />

"Jennifer, what are you doing here? I thought you'd never darken these doors again. You look amazing. Can I take you to dinner?"

"Yes, I'd like that. I wanted to see everyone and tell them goodbye. I'm going to pick up my mother from the hospital in a couple of days, so I need to prepare the guest room for her. I just saw Emily, Jack, and Harry in the day room. I needed that. They saved your life that night, and I wanted to tell them the truth about my brief stay and explain to Harry why I didn't remember him. Do you know what happened to Tara Montgomery, by the way? There's been so much going on that I keep forgetting to ask you. I haven't seen her in group therapy in a while."

"Jennifer, I told you I'd be glad to go with you to Oklahoma City to pick up your mother. Your mother is not going to be up for that long drive. Let's fly and rent a car at the airport, just as we did before. We can get a wheelchair for your mother. She'll probably be weak for a while and maybe even need some physical therapy until she gets her strength back. Let me know. To answer your question, Tara is now living with an aunt again. Her stepfather has been picked up and arrested for attempted rape. She is seeing a therapist to help her deal with the anger she still feels towards her mother. She credits you with giving her the courage to try again for help. She plans to pursue a career in public speaking, travel around the country, share her experiences, and hopes to empower others. She tried to see you before you left, but you had already left Heatherton and were back in your house, and I couldn't reach you."

"Thanks, Tony. I'll definitely take you up on your generous offer. I'm not sure I can manage everything without some help. She'll be released on Thursday if everything goes as planned. That means I should leave by Tuesday at the latest. I'll call you when I get home as soon as I get our tickets. I knew Tara was a strong young woman. I'm sorry I missed her and didn't get to say goodbye. I'm so proud of her. It's funny how I originally came here to find out who murdered my mother, and how so many of the patients I've met here have stolen my heart. I will draft that story and give it my all when things slow down. It will be my best work, leaving Pete at a loss for words, which is a feat in itself.

"I'm so glad you still want to do that. Besides being an outstanding writer, you have a gift, Jennifer. People are naturally drawn to you like a moth to a flame. Many people yearn for love, and it comes naturally to you. People automatically feel better when they're in your presence. The fact that you want to share your experience here speaks volumes. I'm so proud of you, Jen. Against all odds, you have risen like a Phoenix from the ashes. I hope it's not too soon to tell you how I feel about you, as if you didn't already know."

"Thank you for the generous compliments, Tony. I plan to be here for the Christmas party and to say goodbye to everyone. You're right. I have known you for some time. You are a special person, Tony Gallagher, with a sweet soul, and our friendship has always been important to me. I hope you can be patient with me for a while longer, as I am still trying to process everything, and it's a lot."

"Of course, I understand. Take as long as you need. I'm not going anywhere. Please let me know when you have reserved the tickets, and I'll reimburse you. We can leave as soon as you like."

Chapter Sixteen
Clarity from an Unlikely Source

Jennifer, I don't know what to say. I'm speechless. What's so funny? This is the best work you've ever done for our paper." Pete Overton appeared at first meeting to be the quintessential owner and reporter of a local newspaper, right down to his mustache, tight jeans, muscle shirt, shaved head, and the gold chain hanging around his neck. He epitomized an aging hippie who desperately held on to an era long gone. His partying and love of a good beer with a good woman hid a man with a big heart who desperately craved finding that special person to settle down with. The only problem was that he didn't have the slightest idea of how to go about it and would die before he asked anyone for help. "If these characters are real people, it puts a whole new slant on psychiatric hospitals, at least

Heatherton Psychiatric Hospital. I hope you have all the required permission signatures from the patients and the hospital. We don't need any lawsuits coming out of the woodwork. I love how your piece devictimizes the patients, which is rare today and is exactly the kind of news that our readers are starved for. Imagine a place where doctors and staff care about their patients and want them to recover. I love your emphasis on how staff are carefully screened, the uncaring are culled out, and any discovered abuse is reported and subject to prosecution. I'm impressed that you've woven your personal experience into the story. That shows real Moxy. I'm not sure I understand why you would expose yourself to that kind of vulnerability when no one would be the wiser. You've already been through so much. I've been around the block a few times, but I can't believe what a cad Carson turned out to be. You deserve so much more. I always believed you all had the perfect marriage. Jennifer, you have always been like a daughter to me. I've always kept to myself for the most part. I guess I have trust issues. Perhaps that's why I don't connect well with others. My dad was an alcoholic, and my mother was in a drugged stupor as far back as I can remember. I'll never forget hearing my mother screaming hysterically when CPS took me and my little brother away. I grew up in foster homes, but we were separated, and I never saw my little brother again. I guess you could say I raised myself. Big surprise, huh? I'm trying to tell you, please don't let this experience break you. Consider seeking counseling if you need it. I speak from experience. I wasted so many years being angry. It affected every relationship I ever had. Carson is an idiot. I hope they throw the book at him. I know some people you can contact if you need help. No questions asked."

"Thanks, Pete, I appreciate it, but I prefer to let the legal system take care of him; he'll pay. "Carson has already been arrested and is awaiting arraignment. I still want to say a few things to him, but I'll wait for now. Otherwise, I might be tempted to take him out myself. I have considered the exposure I will attract, but if my story helps just one person, it will have achieved its purpose and will be worth it. I appreciate your concern. Don't worry about me, Pete. I have a strong support system. Now I even have my mother back. I'll be fine," she said, giving him a big hug.

"Jennifer, what a pleasant surprise. You look stunning, as usual. Has your mom recovered from the trip? Are you girls getting settled in yet?" How did Pete like your article?"

"Yes, we are. My mother has persuaded me to stay in the house for a while. I was prepared to list it with a realtor, but I suppose there's no hurry now that Carson has been arrested. I'm not sure if Mother can live alone yet, even though she insists she can. Pete loved my article. Can you believe it? I came by to see if I could take you to lunch this time. I saved you a clipping of my article for you to read," she said, laying it on his desk. "Is Pittman's okay?

"Thanks, Jennifer, I can't wait to read it. Pittman's is perfect. I'll get my jacket and drive; you can tell me all about it on the way. You can bring me back to get my car."

Pittman's was a trendy restaurant overlooking a lake in Mandeville, not far from Heatherton. The hospital's doctors, staff, and the evening crowd often frequented it. In addition to its peaceful ambiance, its cuisine was unequaled.

"Tony, I'm having trouble deciding whether to see Tiffany or not." I have too many unanswered questions. If there's even the slightest chance that I can ever forgive her for what she's done, I need the closure so I can move on, but I dread it with every fiber of my being."

I think that's an admirable idea, Jen, but I hope you're prepared for the emotional impact of such a visit; it's likely to be painful. They caught Dr. Aten, by the way. It took a while, but he turned up living in a cabin of one of his relatives in the mountains of Utah. He had a one-way ticket to Balise. He was more than ready to cooperate and sang like a bird. He told the police that he and Edith had colluded and agreed to destroy all files so there would be nothing to tie them to the conspiracy. What he didn't know was that Edith had a different idea. Edith kept your mother's file, including all his notes on the night Eileen supposedly died, that Dr. Denton shared with Dr. Eten. She had been blackmailing him for months. It seems Edith has a serious gambling problem, and she was using Dr. Eten to support her gambling habit. It sounds like her parents were aware of her little problem and told her about it. All her parents' money won't be available until they pass away. Interestingly, she has a trust that isn't accessible until she marries and provides an heir. It's probably a Godsend that she couldn't get her greedy hands on it, as she would have gambled away her entire inheritance by now. Edith and Dr. Aten have a long history together. He also had a record and was a real con artist. Before she double-crossed him and started blackmailing him, they were friends with benefits on and off for years. Something else I found interesting is that your mother had a diamond pendant necklace that Edith had her eye on. She had the background and knew how valuable it was; when she noticed your mother wasn't wearing it anymore, she became obsessed with finding it. No one knew what she planned to do with it, but she spread the word at the hospital and among her patients that someone had stolen it from Eileen. Edith was the one who planted the camera in your room and rifled through your things. She was determined to watch you and monitor how much you knew, but she might have also been looking for the diamond necklace. Both of them will be locked up for a long time. What about Carson? You haven't mentioned his name since he was taken into custody. Are you afraid to be in the house alone when your mom finds a place of her own?"

"Wow! I knew Edith was devious, but clearly, I underestimated her capabilities. She had her greedy hands in everything. No wonder I could feel her hatred for me every time I saw her. The joke's on her. My mother gave the diamond pendant to Emily as a token of their friendship. She wore it under her clothes so no one could see it and would want to steal it. I wonder how Edith was hired at Heatherton in the first place. Don't they do background checks? Never mind, I'm sure they knew how to get around that. Whenever I hear Carson's name, it evokes a range of emotions, the strongest being rage; I want to slam something. I will make that visit as soon as I can. No, I'm not afraid to stay by myself. I'm staying right where I am for now. As for seeing my sister, I'll need to put that on the back burner. We were raised together our whole lives. I'm struggling with the betrayal now."

"Let's see about getting some food in you first," Tony said, handing her a menu.

On the drive home, Jennifer kept thinking about Tony's words. She dreaded seeing Carson and Tiffany, but she needed to face her demons, or she would never be able to heal and move on. *And what about Edith and Dr. Eten?* She shuddered to think what could have happened to her.

Now that Edith, Carson, and Tiffany had been arrested, and it looked like they were not getting out on bail, moving back into her house for the time being was the best thing she could have done. As soon as the doctors released her mother from the hospital, the first thing Jennifer did when she returned to her hotel room was pack up her clothes and personal items she had brought from home, check out, and load her suitcase and makeup bag into the rental car. They all left Oklahoma City and returned home. Eileen moved in with Jennifer. As she and her mother unpacked her belongings and moved her into the guest room, Jennifer was pleasantly surprised by how at peace she felt. Her mother's health was improving steadily every day.

"Jennifer, I'm glad you're home. You just got a call from Heatherton. It was Emily, and she sounded upset. I didn't ask. I don't think she recognized my voice."

"Okay, Mom, thank you. I'll call her back."

"Jennifer, have you heard about Jack?" Emily asked.

"No, what happened? You sound like you've been crying."

"Maybe I can't help it. They say he was sitting by the window like he always does; a car backfired, and he hit the floor. When they got him up, it was like he was in a trance. I guess he was having flashbacks, thought he was back in the war, and shut down. They took him to the hospital last night to make sure he hadn't had a stroke or something. He's back, sitting in the park, but it's as if he isn't there. Perhaps, on some level, he recalls how much he enjoys nature, the outdoors, and being outside. He doesn't seem like Jack anymore. Are you going to go see him?"

"Absolutely, he needs us. I'll catch up with you later. Thank you for letting me know."

Chapter Seventeen
Jack's in Trouble

When Jennifer saw Jack sitting on the bench on the beautiful Heatherton grounds, she almost didn't recognize him. He looked as if he had aged overnight, and the energy surrounding him, like a shroud, was heavy and oppressive.

"Jack, it's Jennifer. How are you?" Only space separated them physically, but emotionally, they were worlds apart. She walked around to face him, trying to initiate eye contact. Only an empty shell of Jack stared back at her. Jennifer fought tears and sat down beside him. "You know, Jack, you need to get well. I hear you have done all the music for all the Christmas parties. I'm looking forward to it. I hope you'll be there; it wouldn't be the same without you. I hope you will save me a dance. Everyone knows you are the best dancer for miles around, so I'll be looking forward to it."

"Emily, I was looking for you. I just saw Jack. I'm so worried about him. He's practically catatonic."

"I feel the same way. There must be some significance surrounding the date because last year, at about the same time, he had an episode. This seems different somehow. It's like he doesn't want to come back this time. I'm going to see if I can get permission from Dr. Gallagher to bring him into the day room and have someone play the piano for us. His favorite is *Rhapsody in Blue*. I know some amazing things have been done for stroke victims with music. Maybe it will help pull him back. Do you want to help me if Dr. Gallagher okays it? Try not to worry; Jack is still in there. We need to keep looking. We can't give up on him now.

"I'd be honored."

As Emily hoped, Dr. Gallagher was more than open to moving Jack into the day room. Much to everyone's surprise, when Emily and Jennifer rolled his wheelchair in, Tony was seated at the piano.

"Dr. Gallagher, I didn't know you played," Emily said.

"A little, certainly not as well as Jack does.

Emily stationed Jack and his wheelchair with his back to the window, where he always sat, so that he could face the piano. His eyes were still blank, and he was as still as an automaton. Dr. Gallagher started playing George Gershwin's *Rhapsody in Blue*. Suddenly, Jack sat up a little straighter and began to hum. Like electricity, the energy in the entire day room transformed, and all eyes were on Jack. Emily and Jennifer started crying. "I knew you were in there, Jack," Emily said, patting him on the shoulder. People came up to shake his hand and hug him as he sat alert in his wheelchair. When Dr. Gallagher finished, Jack stopped humming, but there was life in his eyes as he maneuvered himself over to the piano.

"Dr. Gallagher, I didn't know you played." They visited for a few minutes, with Dr. Gallagher doing most of the talking. Then, he asked Emily to wheel Jack back to his room.

"Jennifer, I'm glad you're back. I need to tell you something. It's been bothering me for a long time. Sit down, darling. When I found your father in the bedroom the night he died, I was devastated. I honestly didn't think I could ever forgive him. I couldn't believe it; it was so out of character for him. I didn't find the note until the following day. It must have fallen out of his hand when the pills kicked in, and it was under the comforter skirt. He had been having an affair for over a year, and he was planning to ask me for a divorce. I guess he couldn't live with the guilt and the breakup of his family. I didn't have a clue. It wasn't a long note; he said he still loved me. It was Marion, his secretary. She was at the funeral, such a cliché. There she was, the dutiful employee, and mistress bawling before God and everyone."

"Oh, Mom, I had no idea. I can't believe you carried this by yourself all these years."

"I can't either. It was the most challenging experience I have ever had in my life. The hardest thing was that he couldn't tell me himself. Instead, he chose the easy way out and left me to clean up his mess. I shudder to think of what would have happened if his life insurance had been canceled. We would have lost everything." Her mother was strong, though, more resilient than any of them realized. Soon, Jennifer was driving her mother around to find a place of her own, despite Jennifer telling her she could stay as long as she liked. Eileen settled on a lovely 1,700-square-foot, two-bedroom, one-and-a-half-bath brick home in a quiet subdivision. She winked at Jennifer and told her the extra bedroom was for her grandchildren to stay in when they came over someday, which was a promising sign of the long road to healing from the ordeal she had endured. With her mom settled and well, Jennifer felt a peace she couldn't explain. Perhaps there was something to the idea that "the truth will set you free." Maybe she could start working on the book she began years ago. Her future had never looked more exciting. She also planned to keep in touch with her friends in Heatherton. According to Emily, Jack was getting better every day.

The Times-Picayune

Page 2, continued
November 2, 2018

Jennifer Nelson,
Reporter

Heatherton,
A Place to Heal

When you hear the words, psychiatric hospital, what are the first adjectives that come to mind? Scary, neglect, isolation, abuse, loneliness, loss of control, and possibly so many others, based on your observation of friends' or loved ones' experiences.
My name is Jennifer Nelson. I am a reporter,

For The Times Picayune. I recently went undercover at Heatherton Psychiatric Hospital to do some research. My mother was a recent patient at Heatherton, and I wanted to learn all I could about daily life there.

Don't let the venerable old buildings fool you the first time you visit Heatherton. Heatherton Psychiatric Hospital has been around for decades. Whatever you do, don't overlook the beautiful grounds. Some of the patients have Contributed their own time and love to their care.

As an undercover reporter, one of the things that impressed me the most was how the

patients at Heatherton
look out for each other.

Heatherton's Patient
Transitional Cabin

I experienced that kind of
loyalty firsthand when I
had an
Anaphylactic reaction to
some shrimp in my
salad, and a
patient immediately
rushed to my side and
called for help.
A doctor on staff
administered
Epinephrine and saved
my life. Everyone has a
different story and faces

unique challenges at Heatherton. Still, whenever they have a bad day or suffer, they are surrounded emotionally by a visit, a shared dessert
Or even a prized trinket. When someone passes away, it is a sad day for all the residents at Heatherton. Initially, I had some preconceived opinions about psychiatric hospitals as well. I attended a Sweethearts Dance during my brief stay at Heatherton. It was a collaborative event. Attendance was amazing. The patients put up all the decorations; the whole event was coordinated and executed by the patients. As for the staff, I was pleasantly surprised to discover that doctors and nurses

sincerely care about their patients at Heatherton. During my short time there, I saw two patients become well enough to return home to their families and re-enter society.

In conclusion, if one of your loved ones suffers from mental illness and needs professional intervention, please call Heatherton Psychiatric Hospital at (504) 123 7654 and make an appointment with one of their doctors. It is one of the healthiest opportunities you can give a loved one to heal in a caring environment.

Chapter Eighteen
The Visit

Jennifer couldn't believe she was following through with a visit to the parish jail to see Carson in less than a month since everything had happened. She ignored the catcalls and loud bangs on the cell bars as a bored security guard led her down a dimly lit hall to a large room, with a chair in each cubicle on the visitor's side, waiting for the inmates to be ushered in on the other side for visitor's hour. When Carson walked in and saw Jennifer, he stopped in his tracks, turned around as if to leave, then changed his mind and came back, sitting down.

"Carson, I assure you, I don't want to see you any more than you want to see me."

"Then, what are you doing here?"

"I'm here because I want to get on with my life. It's called closure. At the very least, could you provide me with some answers? Did you ever love me, or was it only about the money? You slept with my sister and Edith both. Who are you? I always knew you were arrogant, but this is an all-time low for you, Carson. I hope they throw the book at you and Edith both."

"Are you done? Because I am. You and I never jelled; you know that. You have never had to go without anything your entire life, so don't you dare judge me. You have no idea what I went through, fighting and clawing my way to where I am today. And what about Tiffany? She is the ultimate betrayal, isn't she? I bet you didn't see that one coming. Don't think I don't know you've been running all over town with Tony; I'm no fool."

"You are a fool, but I don't care what you think. Is that what this is about? You want me to suffer because you did? You took a brilliant career and threw it all away for your lust for money and women. Was it worth it, Carson? I'm glad I came because you've helped me see the real Carson, and I can finally close that door with relief. You fit the true definition of a narcissist. In Greek mythology, Narcissus was the son of a Greek river god who became so obsessed with his beauty that he spent all his time staring at his reflection in a pool of water. As punishment, he was turned into the narcissus flower named after him. I was so busy catering to your every need throughout our entire marriage that I almost lost my identity. You are the creator of your own destruction.

"Really, Jennifer, so now I'm a flower. You always were a drama queen."

"This conversation is over. I'm done. Good luck, Carson." She didn't even notice the shock on Carson's red face as she quietly got up and walked back down the dim hall from which she had come, but she never looked back.

Jennifer was enjoying the drive to Heatherton for the Christmas party. It had been weeks since she had seen everybody. Everyone would be so surprised that she had brought her mother along. Her heart beat a little faster whenever she thought about Tony being there. She wore a red gown in keeping with the occasion, hoping she wouldn't be overdressed, complete with heels and a matching handbag. Her mother looked lovely in a satin, emerald-green blouse, full-length black skirt, and low-heeled shoes. When they walked into the dayroom together, all eyes were on them. She couldn't believe everything was so festive and wondered how many residents were responsible for the beautiful decorations. A massive white Christmas tree, situated by the piano, was adorned with blue lights and covered in silver and blue balls. The floor had been cleared, and people were already dancing in their finest. She noticed Emily and Harry immediately dancing with big smiles on their faces. When Emily saw Jennifer and her mother, she suddenly stopped, not believing her eyes.

"Eileen, as I live and breathe," she said, running to her and hugging her with tears in her eyes. "I couldn't believe it when I heard the whole story. You look wonderful. Everyone here has fallen in love with your amazing daughter, who has moved mountains to crack this case wide open. I'm delighted to see you looking so well. Come with me. I want to show you off. Do you remember Harry?" Someone in a Santa suit walked toward Jennifer and handed her a small red package wrapped in silver ribbon. "Ho, ho, ho," he said. I hear you've been a good girl this year, Jennifer."

"Jack, I'd know that voice anywhere. It's so good to see you out and about," Jennifer said as she grabbed him and hugged him.

"Thank you." His eyes and matching smile lit up the room, and he hugged Jennifer back with a vengeance. "I hear you're leaving us. I will miss you. I'll never forget you, Jennifer. I appreciate everything you've done for me. Look at that; they match your dress." Jack's little red box contained a pair of small gold bell earrings with miniature red bows.

"Jack, I love them. Excuse me, I need to visit the ladies' room." By the time she reached the restroom, Jennifer was fighting back tears; she was so touched. As she exchanged the earrings she wore for the ones Jack had given her, she marveled again at how close she had become to so many people at Heatherton whom she had only met six months ago.

"Jennifer, you look stunning. May I have this dance? Tony asked. I'm so glad you made it. All eyes are on us, you know. You wouldn't want to disappoint them, would you?"

As Tony swept her away to a lovely waltz, it felt like she was finally where she belonged in his arms.

"Jennifer, I read your article. It's amazing. Your rendering of one of our cabins is beautiful. I never knew you were so talented. I'm so proud of you, and I love how you have represented Heatherton. I knew you made some friends here, but I didn't realize the connection you had formed with our patients."

"I know, and to think my whole intention was to find out who killed my mother. Life is full of surprises. Who is that adorable girl Jack is dancing with? She looks familiar, but I can't quite place her."

That's Barbara Turner; she's a certified nursing assistant here. I'm sure you've noticed that Jack is back; he may be the best I've seen him in a long time. I wouldn't swear to it, but I'm willing to bet Barbara has been a significant influence. They have been an item ever since his last episode. Jack tells me that Barbara starts nursing school in the spring. He is moving in with her after the holidays. She has a large house in Mandeville that she inherited from her father. He will be continuing his therapy here and transitioning out as an outpatient. I think he might make it this time."

"I'm getting goosebumps. That's amazing; what wonderful news. I remember her now. She introduced herself to me right after I moved in. She seemed like a nice person. What about his PTSD?"

"He'll never be cured. He'll have to live with PTSD for the rest of his life. You know now that an episode can be brought on by something as innocuous as a car backfiring or the smell of a bonfire that throws him right back into the trauma he experienced in the war. We can teach him to recognize the triggers and how to manage his episodes better, but his brain has been hardwired by what happened to him. I believe that falling in love with someone is one of the best things that can happen to them. He has a reason to want to get better. The fact that she is in the medical field is an added benefit.

"I'm so happy for him. Who knows, maybe we'll be attending a wedding someday."

"I agree. I think that's a definite possibility. So where does that leave us?"

"Us?"

"Yes, you already know how I feel about you; I've been in love with you for a long time. I want to spend the rest of my life with you, Jennifer. It's up to you if that's what you want."

"That's exactly what I want. I love you, too, Tony. I thought you'd never ask," she said, snuggling closer into his arms. "It might be better to wait until I'm officially divorced, don't you think?"

"So, Mother, did you have a good time? Emily was ecstatic to see her dear friend again. It looks like she and Harry have fallen in love. They are perfect for each other."

"I had a wonderful time. I'm so happy for Emily. She has a good heart and deserves it. Speaking of love, Tony is head over heels in love with you, honey. He didn't take his eyes off you the whole night. I think the feeling is mutual, isn't it?"

"Yes, I have fallen for Tony hard. I fought it, but he was irresistible. I am just afraid to trust again after Carson."

"I get that, but you must move on. Life is too short to allow someone like Carson to ruin your life."

"Speaking of Carson, you have a letter here from Carson," she said, picking it up off a pile of mail on the floor from the mail slot. I know that we originally planned to have a girls' sleepover and talk all night, but I think I will turn in. It's been a while since I've danced like that. I'm exhausted. Tomorrow is a big day for me. I'm going shopping for patio furniture."

Jennifer shoved Carson's unopened letter into the desk drawer as she watched her mother climb the stairs to bed. *I'll deal with that later. Whatever it is, it can wait.*

Jennifer was surprised by how much she missed her mother. She was grateful her mother was safe and settled in her new home. It was surreal how much had happened between them in such a short time, and she was ecstatic that she even had her mother back when she believed she was dead for two years. It was a miracle. She was putting some bath salts in the bathtub and looking forward to a hot bath when she thought she heard a noise coming from the back door in the kitchen. She quickly turned the water off and grabbed her robe. She was headed for the kitchen when suddenly she received a blow to the back of her head. Everything went black, and she hit the floor like a ton of bricks. The first thing Jennifer saw when she came to was Edith Parker leaning over her with a gun pointed at her forehead. Simultaneously, she realized she was sitting on her kitchen chair with her feet tied and her hands bound behind her back.

What are you doing here, Edith? You're supposed to be in jail. How did you get in?"

"Questions, questions, so many questions. That nose of yours is what gets you in so much trouble in the first place. I still don't like your attitude. I couldn't believe you kept an extra key under the doormat. It always amazes me how oblivious people can be. I would have expected more of you. It does help to have financial backing and establish connections with influential individuals. My parents pulled a few favors and bailed me out."

"So why are you here instead of long gone? It's not like you care about leaving your parents holding the bag. I assumed you had already headed off for parts unknown."

"That's right, I don't care. I have some debt obligations, but they won't loan me any money to help me. I never thought my parents would throw me under the bus when I needed them the most."

"You mean they wouldn't pay your gambling debts anymore? So, why are you really here? My only asset is this house; we both know you don't have much time to wait around."

"Believe what you like. I'm here because I want the diamond pendant your mom stopped wearing; I know you have it. I grew up very wealthy and know that necklace is worth a great deal; I need some fast cash.

"Really? What makes you think I have it? Have you forgotten my mother was with you and my husband, and in a drugged stupor for the last two years? I haven't a clue. You must be desperate. I wouldn't tell you even if I knew where it was. Why would I? You put a camera in my room, stole my artwork for the paper, and tried to kill me twice. It was you who pushed me down the stairs."

"I guess you're smarter than I gave you credit for, Edith said, releasing the safety on the gun so Jennifer would hear it. Suddenly, the gun went off, and Jennifer felt a shot whiz by her, just missing her arm as Edith landed at her feet with Tony on top of her as he wrestled her for the gun. The gun slid across the floor, and Tony was able to grab it before Edith knew what had happened.

"Jen, are you okay? I thought you might feel lonely with your mom gone, so I wanted to surprise you with some Chinese food. Imagine my surprise when I heard Edith's voice through the front door, and I managed to call the police. There they are," he said, still holding the gun on Edith and motioning her towards the front door.

The police were more than happy to snap handcuffs on her when they met her at the door.

"Guess what? I might have to make us an omelet. Your Chinese food is all over the front porch where I dropped it. Where's your broom and a dustpan?"

⁂

The parish jail Tiffany was held in while awaiting her trial wasn't much different from most jails. A retired military officer managed it, and it showed. It was run like a tight ship, noticeably clean, and visiting hours were 11:00 a.m. and 7:00 p.m., sharp, with no exceptions, and each visit lasted a maximum of one hour. When Jennifer saw Tiffany in the family visiting room, she hardly recognized her. She had lost at least fifteen pounds, and her face had developed some stress lines she hadn't had before. Jennifer sat at the table across from her sister at a total loss, wondering what to say. She had to ask herself why she was even there in the first place.

"Tiffany, I don't know where to start. Help me understand how you could do this to our mother, let alone to yourself.

"I wouldn't expect you to understand. We might share the same DNA and look alike, but that's where it stops. We are as different as our fingerprints in every way. Even when we were kids, you always had all the advantages in school, the most popular boyfriends, straight A's, and you could do no wrong as far as Mom was concerned."

"Really, Tiffany, you're playing the 'victim card.' Why am I not surprised?"

Tiffany was crying by now. You never listen to me. I always picked boyfriends who were losers. Mom said I was always attracted to the wrong kind of men. I was just like our father, with a skewed moral compass. I don't know if that's true, but I never intended to get involved with Carson; I have to live with that, but I thought he loved me. I've made bad decisions all my life, but it's as if he had some crazy power over me. I lost myself completely. I realize now he was using me to get Mom's money. I'll never be able to make it up to you or Mom, but maybe I can get some help while I'm here. I know you don't believe me, but I'm sorry. Is Mom okay?"

"What are you talking about? Did you know about the letter Dad left?"

"Yes, you know I was always Daddy's little girl, and Mom could never do anything with me. We were like water and oil. After he died, I used to sneak up to their bedroom to play. It made me feel close to him somehow. I found the letter. One day, I was sitting on the bed reading and saw something white sticking out from under the nightstand. It was a note from Dad to Mom. When I read it, I was furious with him. I took it to Mom and demanded an explanation. She knew nothing about it. Of course, she was crushed and refused to talk about it. Later, whenever I tried to ask her about it, she would shut me down. After a while, I gave up and quit asking. I guess I don't have a moral compass, either. Maybe it's in my DNA."

"Tiffany, that's a cop-out. Mom just told me. She protected you even then, saying she found it under the bed skirt. I had no idea. Dad was weak. He took the easy way out rather than face his demons. I can't imagine the toll that finding that letter must have taken on you, but you're not weak. You made some terrible choices, but you still have options. We all do. You let yourself be influenced and controlled by Carson. You're right. Carson was using you. That's what he does. Look how many years it took me to see past the mask. You can choose to pull yourself together and seek counseling. No one can do it for you. Mom's fine. She has been completely evaluated and has no dementia. She's never been better. She's just found a place, is living by herself, and doing well. That should come as no surprise. Tony said you didn't know anything about Edith and Carson, nor did Edith know anything about your relationship with Carson. Edith played a major role in keeping Mom in a constant state of tumult and drugging her so she would be diagnosed with dementia, but you played a part in perpetuating that. I haven't spoken with Edith yet, but I haven't decided whether I ever want to. I hope she is prosecuted to the fullest extent of the law. Did you know her parents pulled some strings and got her out of jail? She broke into my house the other night and hit me over the head hard enough to knock me out. When I woke up, she was standing over me with a gun pointed at my forehead, and I was tied to a chair. She has a serious gambling problem and was after Mom's diamond pendant. She was desperate for some fast cash. I guess she was under pressure because of her gambling debts, and her parents refused to help her anymore. If Tony hadn't shown up and taken the gun away from her, there's no telling what would have happened. He saved my life twice. She's back in jail where she belongs."

"I had no idea. Jennifer, I'm so sorry. Whether you believe it or not, I was giving Mom the meds that Edith prescribed to her, but I truly thought she had dementia. That should tell you how much power Carson had over me. I would never have believed what Edith tried to do if I hadn't heard it myself, and now I hear this. I never liked her, but I was unaware of her capabilities. She's a monster. Nor would I have believed Carson was capable of trying to murder you. I knew he was obsessed with money, but I never imagined the lengths he was willing to go to. Does Mom hate me? Will I ever see her or you again?"

"Yes, Edith's a monster, and so is Carson. I can't speak for Mom; that's something you'll need to work out between the two of you." Jennifer was crying as well. "I will be back. Get some help, Tiffany, and find out what brought you here in the first place. You'll never be able to forgive yourself otherwise and move on. Their quick hug was immediately interrupted when a guard bellowed, 'No touching.' On the ride home, Jennifer reflected on all the steps that had led up to this moment and could feel the long-needed closure circling her like a warm blanket. She had one more thing she needed to do.

The next morning, Jennifer was shocked when Tiffany called and told her that Edith and Carson were also being arraigned first thing Monday morning. She wasn't looking forward to seeing them all again, but was anxious to put it all behind her.

"Tony, you can't be serious. You don't have to accompany me to court on Monday."

"I wouldn't think of doing anything else. I'm here for you because I want to be, Jen."

Jennifer was experiencing a wide range of conflicting emotions when she and Tony entered the courtroom. If Tony hadn't been with her, she might have been tempted to turn around and leave. She was grateful for his support. No sooner had they been seated when a deputy ushered in Carson. It was surreal to see him in handcuffs.

"All rise. This court, presided over by the Honorable Judge McGowan, is now in session. Please be seated and come to order."

"Mr. Nelson, it is my understanding, based on information from Mr. Thomas, your attorney, that you have entered a guilty plea to all charges." Is that correct?"

"Yes, your honor, I have."

I must ask you, has anyone pressured or coerced you in any way to make this decision?

"No, your honor, they haven't."

"Do you understand that you waive your constitutional right to a trial by pleading guilty to these charges?"

"Yes, your honor, I do."

Lynn G. Armstrong

Chapter Twenty
Another Surprise

Very well, Mr. Nelson, a sentencing hearing is set for Monday at 9:00 a.m., one week from today. No bail is set. Bailiff, will you please escort Mr. Nelson out? We will take a brief break."

"Boy, I didn't see that coming," Tony whispered to Jennifer as they found a bench outside the courtroom and sat down. Sitting through Carson's arraignment was one thing, but seeing Tiffany in the courtroom before the judge was awkward and unbearable. When they escorted Tiffany from the courtroom, Jennifer was allowed to hug Tiffany briefly. They both cried.

"Tony, I'm ready to leave. I don't care what happens to Edith. Let's go."

As they walked back to Tony's car, he said. "I wouldn't worry too much about Edith Parker. Evil has many faces. She is a master of improvisation and loyal to no one. I heard from Officer Britton that she already has two guards vying for her affections for whatever she needs, and she hasn't even been sentenced yet. Before I forget, Tara Montgomery called me to give me her new number. She wants you to call her for lunch so you girls can catch up."

A week later, Tiffany called Jennifer and told her that it seemed that Edith had a record. No one knew how she ever got a job in another hospital again. Years ago, in Ohio, she was charged and convicted of negligent health endangerment of one of her patients by overmedicating her. The woman died of complications brought on by the negligence, and Edith served a two-year sentence. Because of her previous crime, Judge McGowan sentenced her to seven years without the possibility of parole. This time, her parents couldn't buy her freedom, and she would have plenty of time to think about what she had done. Tiffany received one year and six months of probation due to her clean record. Carson accepted his lawyer's offer and received a five-year sentence with the possibility of parole; his medical license was also suspended indefinitely. It would be a long time before he ever practiced medicine again. If ever.

When Jennifer got off the phone, she was overwhelmed by the myriad of emotions she was experiencing. On the one hand, she was relieved that Carson, Edith, and Tiffany were being held accountable for their crimes. On the other hand, she knew it would take years to get over the heartbreak Carson and her sister had caused her, if ever. It would require a great deal of prayer. Suddenly, she remembered Carson's letter, realized she had forgotten it, and retrieved it from the desk drawer.

Jennifer,

I imagine I'm the last person you ever expected to hear from. I can't ever justify what I have done to you, your mother, or even Tiffany, as she was also a victim. I don't expect you ever to forgive me, but I want you to know that nothing you ever did influenced anything I did. I take full responsibility for all the pain I've caused you and your family. You are a good woman, Jennifer, and you were a good wife. I don't know what makes me do the things I do. I'm getting therapy while I'm here, and maybe I'll find out so I can get on with my life, whatever that is.

Please consider keeping the house for a while. It is worth a great deal, and now isn't the best time to sell until the market picks up. If you don't mind, would you pack up some of my things and put them in the basement for a while? Email me if you have any questions. I'm sorry about everything. I heard what Edith did to you. Don't worry about her bothering you again. She'll be locked up for a long time. She even fooled me. I received your divorce petition. I'll sign the divorce papers and any other documents you'd like, within reason. Please have your lawyer contact Barry; I'll review everything and have Barry get back to your lawyer.

Carson

Jennifer was sitting in Benny's, an upscale restaurant near the university frequented by the younger crowd and many students. She had reached Tara Montgomery at her new number and looked forward to connecting with her again.

"Tara, you look terrific! Yellow is definitely your color."
Tara wore a blue floral-print chiffon dress with a
handkerchief hem and a yellow blazer."

"So do you, but you always look elegant. I'm so glad
we could meet for lunch since I didn't get a chance to
say goodbye before you left. There were many stories
about why you left, but I know better than anyone that
you can rarely believe what you hear firsthand. Did your
leaving have anything to do with Edith Parker? No one
likes that woman."

"She definitely was a part of it, but not the way you
would think. Let me start at the beginning. I don't think
you were at Heatherton when my mother, Eileen
Bastille, lived there. She had been diagnosed with
dementia, and most of the time, she was incoherent and
barely able to function. Edith Parker was her nurse, and
some of the residents thought she was overmedicated
because she would occasionally pretend she had taken
her meds when she hadn't and be quite lucid. I am
actually a reporter working for The Times Picayune and
have been living at Heatherton undercover for a few
months, trying to figure out what happened to my
mother. One day she was fine, and the next morning I
was called and told she had died in her sleep. Are you
okay, Tara? You look pale."

"I'm fine. I can see you as a reporter, but I'm just a little
surprised. Please go on."

"It took a while to get to the bottom of everything, but
it was a massive conspiracy between Dr. Nelson, my
husband, Edith Parker, and my twin sister Tiffany. After
they reported her death, they took her to Oklahoma, and

she has been living there for two years with my sister. They've all been arrested and sentenced. Miraculously, my mother was alive, and once she was taken off her meds, she was as good as new. It has been a great shock for my mother and me, and we are still grieving for the betrayal. Hopefully, I haven't completely freaked you out. How are you doing since you left Heatherton?"

"Wow, that's a lot, but I think I always knew there was something special about you. You must be ecstatic to have your mom back. You have done so much for me. You gave me the confidence to believe in myself when no one else did, and I've been able to regain control of my life. My stepfather has been arrested and charged with attempted rape and child endangerment. There is no statute of limitations in this state. My mother was exonerated for her complicity by being a witness for the prosecution. I have an apartment and am going to UNO. I still see a therapist as an outpatient every other month. I'm majoring in communication and have a minor in psychology. As a public speaker, I plan to travel the country to make others like me aware that they have options and to pursue their dreams."

"Tara, I'm so proud of you. That is wonderful," she said, grabbing her and hugging her. I hope you'll let me know when you start so I can be there."

"Absolutely."

<hr>

Tony, what are you doing here? I was going to call you. I have some great news. Carson has agreed to sign my divorce papers. I'll finally be free to close that door and get on with my life."

"That is fantastic news. Let me take you out to Commander's Palace to celebrate."

"That's a pretty fancy place to celebrate a divorce. Tony……"

"I know you're not officially divorced, but I don't want to risk you getting away. Jennifer, will you marry me?" Tony said, opening a ring box that contained an exquisite ring, which captured the overhead lighting from within and sparkled in all its splendor. Please say yes; my knee is killing me. This was my grandmother's ring. We can always have the jeweler make any adjustments or changes you like."

"No, it is the most beautiful ring I've ever seen. I love it exactly the way it is. Yes, I'll marry you, she said as he immediately slipped the ring on her finger."

"Well, look at that. It's a perfect fit," he said as he pulled her into his arms and kissed her.

The End

Acknowledgments

There are always so many people who contribute to the compilation of a book. Without them, the finished product could never have come to fruition, and *Betrayal* has been no exception. I want to thank Peggy Brown, MSW, LSW, for writing the foreword in my book. I am so honored by her contribution, which I greatly appreciate.

I got the idea for Betrayal one day while working on *Julia's Odyssey*, jotted down some notes, and put them aside. Sometime later, I was a guest at the house of Margie Monteleone, a dear friend, at a writer's club meeting. I spoke with Lucinda Beecham, a friend from years ago, about the psychiatric thriller and how I would like to tour a psychiatric hospital and possibly take some pictures of its buildings for the book cover. The old Southeast Mandeville Psychiatric Hospital came up in our conversation, and I immediately knew it would be perfect. What a tribute to that venerable, historic old building! Thanks to Joe Buckley, CEO of Northlake Behavioral Health System, I obtained permission to take the much-wanted pictures and tour its buildings. It was worth the wait, I assure you. Thanks, Lucinda, for a great idea. While *Betrayal* takes place at Heatherton Psychiatric Hospital, a fictitious psychiatric hospital, I was so impressed with Southeast Mandeville Psychiatric Hospital's rich history that I want to acknowledge the warm welcome I received from Mr. Joe Buckley, Kylie, his assistant, and the delightful Ms. Cora Toler. What impressed me the most was the empathy and pride in their voices as they shared their experiences. The day I met Mr. Buckley, I brought my son, Jim Schroeder, and his lovely wife, Donna, with me to take pictures. Due to privacy concerns, we toured some of the original historic buildings that opened their doors in 1942 but are now no longer in use. I found it fascinating. Later, I conducted a telephone interview with Cora Toler. As Mr. Buckley said, she had worked at Northlake Behavior Health System since 1985 and was an excellent source of information. She worked directly with patients for over twenty-five years and has provided various services in other departments. I enjoyed interviewing her. You couldn't help but hear her compassion for her patients as she spoke. We all have experiences that sometimes necessitate seeking help to get back on our path. Mental health could never be more important than it is today. I couldn't finish my book without including a tribute to Northlake Behavioral Health System, a venerable monument to mental health in Louisiana for eighty-two years. Congratulations to Mr. Joe Buckley and his amazing staff.

Thanks to my friend, Mara Gulledge, Web Developer with Aram Technologics. She is always there for me, cheering me on.

Thanks to my dear friends and family for sticking with me for this book. I have never encountered so many distractions or technical challenges in the development of any of my books before, and I couldn't have done so without the support of friends and family.

The old Mandeville Psychiatric Hospital
Look at those automobiles.

Author's Notes

"I want to thank my readers for reading *Betrayal*. I hope you enjoyed it as much as I enjoyed writing it for you. It reminds us that our spirit can prevail no matter what happens to us. It is one of our finest attributes that defines our humanness."

Betrayal can be found on creationsbylynn.org, my website and bookstore, as well as an e-book on Amazon.com, Barnes & Noble.com, and Lulu.com, or at Bayou Booksellers in Hammond, LA. You can also purchase *Betrayal* directly from my inventory.

Remember, you can leave a review for me on my website, Amazon, or any of the other platforms mentioned above. Reviews are a valuable tool, enabling authors to connect with their readers and produce more effective books. Please follow me on my website to stay updated on the release date of my next book, Redemption. I'm excited about it. It will be my first Christian book. If you enjoyed *The Sword Cuts Both Ways and Julia's Odyssey, I'm planning a prequel* in the series, but that will be a little later. Please visit my website and share your thoughts. I'd love to hear from you.

Book Club Meeting Questions

1. What did you think of Jennifer's idea to go undercover in a psychiatric hospital? Could you have done it under her circumstances?
2. What did you think about Carson's response to her idea?
3. Overall, did you think the patients at Heatherton Psychiatric Hospital were treated well?
4. What did you think of Edith Parker, Jennifer's nemesis?
5. Did you think Jennifer's mother was murdered?
6. Did you figure out that Jennifer was a twin? At what point in the story?
7. Did you ever suspect Carson wasn't a particularly good person? Were you shocked when his true character was exposed?
8. How would you have dealt with Carson in Jennifer's situation?
9. Were you able to make an emotional connection to Jack Hale? Emily Petito? Harry Mason?
10. What did you like or dislike about this story? Would you like to read more stories like this?
11. Do you believe there is still a stigma regarding mental health in our community?

www.ingramcontent.com/pod-product-compliance
Lightning Source LLC
Chambersburg PA
CBHW030548030726
47495CB00004B/1182